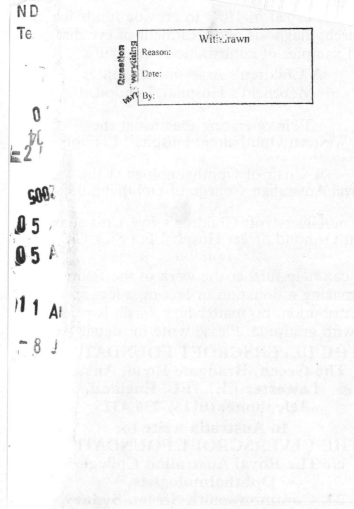

MAN WITHOUT A YESTERDAY

Robbed of his memory by a head wound, Johnny No Name finds himself lost in the Black Hills of Dakota, where bounty hunters see in him a quick chance of reward. He is held captive by Holy Jack, a religious zealot, whose nineteen-year-old daughter turns to Johnny for help. Together, they are hounded by her irate father, bounty hunters, hostile Sioux and even the law. As Johnny fights for his life, fate leads him towards a startling discovery.

MARK BANNERMAN

MAN WITHOUT A YESTERDAY

Complete and Unabridged

LINFORD
Leicester

First published in Great Britain in 1998 by
Robert Hale Limited
London

First Linford Edition
published 1999
by arrangement with
Robert Hale Limited
London

British Library CIP Data

Lewing, Anthony
    Man without a yesterday.—Large print ed.—
    Linford western library
    1. Western stories
    2. Large type books
    I. Title
    823.9'14 [F]

    ISBN 0–7089–5515–0

Published by
F. A. Thorpe (Publishing) Ltd.
Anstey, Leicestershire

Set by Words & Graphics Ltd.
Anstey, Leicestershire
Printed and bound in Great Britain by
T. J. International Ltd., Padstow, Cornwall

This book is printed on acid-free paper

For Peter Reese,
My Partner on the Trail

1

He rose through a dream world like a drowning man palming aside tendrils of weed as he struggled towards the surface. Then the fog in his mind turned red; sightless consciousness came, and with it an echoing sound like chalk being dragged across a blackboard. He tried to open his eyes but he hadn't enough strength. His lids felt leaden, swollen. The smell of earth seemed almost suffocating. Where am I? he wondered. He did not know. He could not remember.

Pain started.

It throbbed through the left side of his head, moving down his cheekbone and jaw, into his neck and shoulders. Its intensity increased. He wondered if he had been scalped — or perhaps his skull had been split and his brains were leaking. He groaned.

1

At last he managed to open his right eye, the light stinging like salt, causing him to blink. Something was crawling over his face. He twitched instinctively and a big fly rose up, buzzing angrily. His left eye remained shut. Above him, he could see blue sky margined by walls of earth. He was lying on his back in a narrow pit about two feet deep. It was the shape of a grave. It had not been dug by an expert, but hacked into the earth by some layman.

He made another discovery: the scraping sounds he had heard were the cries of crows, high in branches. Am I in Hell? Have my sins been so bad that this is my eternal fate? But he could not remember committing sins. In fact, he could not remember anything — not even his name.

Working his shoulders, he managed to move his arms; they had been partially covered with earth. It was as if the gravedigger had grown bored with his work and had given up long before it was completed. His strength was seeping back, somehow enabling him to fight his pain and raging headache. With teeth gritted, he rolled on to his side. Stricken by trembling, he experienced a spasm of fear. He calmed himself, then, with his fingers, he rubbed his left eye. It was crusted with blood but he eased it open by tugging at his eyelash. Next, he slid his hands over the rim of the trench, hauled himself to his knees and squinted around.

He was on a hillside, verdant and green in the sunshine, speckled with flowers and closely bordered by trees. Through these he glimpsed the lighter snow-tipped peaks of granite crags. Turning, he peered downwards, seeing tier upon tier of hilltops, dark-forested slopes and deep valleys, all stretching away into an infinity of sky, heat-haze and distance. He felt dwarfed by immensity. What was this place? How had he got here? Why was this headache driving him crazy?

Gingerly, he reached up, felt a moistness and knew he was bleeding.

He probed his head with gentle fingers, and satisfied himself that he had not been scalped, that the skull was not split and that his brains were still encased. His face was puffy.

Anger stirred him. Why had this happened? Who had treated him so? He straightened up, hoisted his leg out of the trench and dragged himself clear. He crouched in grass, leaning against the pile of excavated earth, and took stock. He realized he was alone. Or at least there was nobody around he could see.

Questions jabbed at him but he had no answers. All he had was a premonition that danger was pressing in, that so far mere luck had enabled him to cling to life, that soon he would have to confront some enemy.

His mouth felt like dry parchment. He must find a stream.

He was wearing a coarse, cotton-like suit which was grimy and torn; he noticed its regular markings — arrowheads stamped into the cloth. He suspected that he had committed some fearful crime. But why wasn't he behind bars, and would he be judged guilty if he could not recall what he had done?

$$\star \quad \star \quad \star$$

It had been two days since Otis had examined the chain that shackled him to the two other convicts, Will Selby and Grinner Willoughby. The three convicted men were being transported by wagon along the trail south of the Black Hills to the newly built penitentiary at Canby City. The chain ran through rings on the handcuffs they wore. The key to the heavy-duty padlock which secured it, together with the keys to the handcuffs, was on a bunch attached to the belt of Chief Prison Officer Niles Turner.

'Gettin' them keys away from him,' Grinner Willoughby murmured to Otis, 'would be like tryin' to open a can of beans with bare fingers.'

Otis nodded. He was thirty-eight

years old, had a craggy face with a jaw thickened with rust-coloured beard. His nose had a kink in it, halfway up; it had been broken long ago and left to heal itself.

Right now his nerves were tingling.

For the hundredth time, he studied his surroundings: the canvas-topped wagon in which they were seated; the four men guarding them; the big-bored Springfield rifle each held.

He knew that following close behind was another wagon, which contained additional armed guards. He also knew that they were trundling along some twenty miles south of the Black Hills, South Dakota. His stocky body ached from the hours of jolting discomfort.

'I guess,' Will Selby remarked, leaning in close, 'that all this security is a compliment to our reputations.' Selby was a six-foot iron-muscled man, a Southerner like Willoughby, of about forty. There was something primitive about his face with its protruding brow ridges and heavy jaw. His next words

6

came as a whisper. 'One thing's for sure. I'm not gonna spend the rest of my life behind bars.'

'Prison Service ain't takin' no chances with us,' Willoughby remarked. At Shiloh, a bullet had caught his cheekbone and somehow widened his mouth. This had given him a simpleton's grin, and he often adopted a seemingly inane and questioning manner, though in truth his brain was sharp. Otis knew that he'd served with Selby in the Civil War, existing on a knife edge as they'd spied on troop positions behind Union lines. Afterwards, neither man had taken to the tame existence offered in the post-war South; so, together, they had sought opportunities beyond the law, gradually becoming more daring. Over seven years, they had successfully robbed stage-coaches, banks and trains. Finally had come the massive payroll strike. They had made a mockery of the law and those who sought to catch them — until disaster struck.

★ ★ ★

The spring day had cooled into evening and Niles Turner called a halt close to the Cheyenne River, here only twenty yards wide. The prison officers climbed from the wagons. Otis listened to them talking as they unhitched the mules.

'Hope there ain't no Injuns around.'

'They'd be crazy to trouble a well-armed party like ours.'

'Injuns'll only get riled up if we blunder into their precious Black Hills, and we won't do that.'

Shortly the mules were led down to the river.

Niles Turner ordered his three prisoners to follow suit. 'No lingerin',' he grunted as he lit a cigarette, 'and don't you try anythin' funny. Wouldn't grieve me if scum like you didn't make it to that new luxury accommodation!'

Otis and his two companions clambered from the wagon, moving clumsily because of the linking chain. They stretched their legs and gazed around at

8

the vast, lonesome terrain. The clouds were dark, their undersides streaked with purple and pink which lay reflected in the river; dusk was creeping in over the hills on the far side of the water, making the cloaking forest look black.

Another officer, a vole-faced, skinny youngster called Evans, joined Turner and the prisoners as they moved to the water. Turner didn't choose the same point as the remaining guards and mules were using, instead, he angled slightly downstream, selecting a small inlet that lay at the mouth of a gulch. To reach it they passed between big boulders and descended a steep bank. It was convenient enough; it kept the prisoners closely together — but it was shielded from the view of the other guards.

Otis drew the smoke from Turner's cigarette into his nostrils. *It must be now*, he thought. He contrived a wistful look, forcing a calmness into his voice as he turned towards Turner. 'It fair sickens me to see you puffing away

9

and me gasping so.'

Niles Turner hesitated, then he nodded. 'You can have a couple o' draws, no more.' He stepped across to Otis and transferred the cigarette to his lips.

At that moment, Turner's right hip was pushed towards Otis — and with it, his loosely holstered Navy Colt. In a flash, Otis snatched the pistol clear of its leather. Thumbing back the hammer, he thrust it into Turner's belly, snarling at him to raise his hands and keep his mouth shut. Turner unleashed an obscenity, glanced furtively around for help but saw none. He raised his hands. Seeing his chance, Will Selby leaned across and, despite his cuffed wrists, extracted Evans's gun from its holster. He held it levelled inches from the youngster's incredulous face.

'The keys!' Otis demanded.

Ashen faced, the senior prison officer lowered his hands and unclasped the keys from his belt.

Willoughby, grinning like a clown,

was for once speechless, but his eyes were wide with excitement as Otis took charge of the keys and unfastened the chain, followed by the handcuffs. Within seconds, all three convicts were free.

Selby grabbed young Evans by the arm and spoke to Turner, his mean words coming with the deadliness of a rattler's warning. 'Come after us and the kid's a dead'un. I swear it!'

Turner registered frustration with a tremulous sigh, then he nodded his grudging understanding.

Otis led the frantic rush as the convicts took to their heels. They followed the course of the river, keeping below the shoulder of the bank, scrambling through fallen timber and rocks. Otis glanced back and saw how Selby was keeping an iron grip on the wide-eyed Evans, forcing him unmercifully forward.

Presently they pulled up, fighting back their breath to listen. There was no indication of pursuit.

'They know we'll damn well kill the

kid if they give chase,' Selby muttered.

Evans had dropped any pretence of bravado now. 'I won't cause no trouble. Don't hurt me. My ma's old; she needs my support.'

Willoughby panted, 'For God's sake, let's get goin' before they change their minds an' give chase!'

'Yeah.' Otis led the way as they ran on. With darkness coming they reached a fording point and splashed across to the far side. Thereafter, they left the river and cut northward through shadowy willows and cottonwood, the trunks of the trees gradually merging into deeper gloom of night. Selby had strapped Evans to his arm with a leather belt. The young prison officer was gasping for breath, stumbling and slowing their progress. Selby's patience was growing thin.

Willoughby had moved ahead as they reached higher ground, with Otis close behind him and, further back, Selby with his hostage. Otis was considering that maybe they should let Evans go, that the youth could do them neither harm nor good now, but suddenly the sharp snap of a pistol shot sounded.

Both Willoughby and Otis pulled up, glancing back, then Selby joined them. He was holding the leather belt. 'No point in draggin' that kid along no more.'

Otis felt stunned. 'You didn't . . . ?'

Selby spat into the darkness. 'Sure I did. With his own damned gun!'

'There was no need to kill him,' Willoughby said.

Selby's anger came sharply. 'I make the decisions here. If that ain't good enough, you know what you can do!'

Willoughby shook his head, but he backed down. 'No offence, Will. I guess you know best.'

Otis watched in silence. He felt sickened, but he was not prepared to face Selby's wrath — not yet.

Selby stripped off the clothing from the body. He tossed the coat to Willoughby and put the rest on over his prison garb. It was a tight fit. He strapped the kid's gunbelt about his waist. It was slotted with shells. He'd already extracted a knife. Now he placed both pistol and knife in their respective scabbards. 'Let's get the body hid,' he grunted.

Otis felt his gaze drawn to the corpse, sprawled there pale and naked. He could see the darkness down the side of the face where the bullet had caused blood to spurt out — but it was the eyes that distressed him: they showed clearly in the moonlight, wide open and frozen in terror. He had seen the same look in the eyes of other dead folk and it always made him uneasy.

He leaned over and thumbed down Evans's eyelids, shutting away that final panic, then they dragged the body to the side and covered it with rocks, spreading leaves and foliage so as to throw any trackers off the scent.

Otis bitterly regretted the killing of this boy; it had not been necessary. It only served to augment previous crime, to bring it to a level which invited but one punishment — the hangrope.

In silence, they pressed on through the darkness, until eventually they came clear of the forest and reached a razorback ridge. Here, exhausted, they took rest. The stars and full moon were bright, silvering the close-in land with mysterious softness. The night air was cold and punctuated by the eerie calls of wild creatures. Otis shivered, his sweat-sodden prison-suit chilling him. Ahead, the Black Hills loomed like brooding dark ghosts, blocking off the lighter sky.

Again he reminded himself that these hills were sacred to the Indians, the centre of the Lakota Hoop, an unmapped wilderness so far forbidden to the whites — a place of ancient spirits.

Luck favoured them; they scared a small deer from the brush, setting it scampering into the moonlit open. Otis rested his pistol across his forearm and fired a single shot, never dreaming that the bullet would strike home. To his astonishment the kill was clean. They skinned the animal and roasted it over the fire Selby lit with the matches he'd found in the pocket of Evans's coat.

They'd made their camp in a hollow beneath the crest of the ridge outcrop. Crouching about the embers, their hunger satisfied, Otis glanced at his companions. He felt he could trust Willoughby, but he knew that Selby was as dangerous as a powder-keg. Even so, there was something Otis had to know.

He licked the grease from his fingers and enquired, 'Where we headed? You seem sure set on the way we're going.'

Selby exchanged glances with Willoughby. The latter said, 'You might as well tell him, Will. He's one of us now. He did us a good turn by grabbin' Turner's gun. He's proved hisself a useful fella to have around. Anyway, in this country, three's better'n two, that's for sure.'

Selby pondered on things, his brow furrowed. At last he seemed to make up his mind because he nodded. Maybe he'd heeded Willoughby's words, maybe not. Maybe he just figured it was best to keep Otis where he could watch him — and close enough at hand to dispose of him, when the mood struck, in the same way he had Evans. Even so, his voice came amenably enough. 'You probably heard we did a big cash job before we got caught.'

'Sure,' Otis said. 'A real clever job, I guess.'

'Well,' Selby went on, 'it's mighty fortunate we made our break near the Black Hills. That's where we hid the pay-roll cash after we ambushed that stage. That's where we're headed now. We'll take enough of that cash for our immediate needs and come back later for the rest, when the hue and cry's died a death.'

Otis said, 'The Injuns won't take kindly to intrusion.'

Selby laughed. 'They sure won't, but if we're lucky they won't know we're around. In a way, it's the safest place for us to be, 'cos no whites'll fancy riskin' their scalps by comin' after us.'

Otis smiled. 'Makes sense.'

Presently, they let the fire die and rested down. They had many miles yet to cover, and they would have to be vigilant every inch of the way.

But Otis lay awake. Willoughby was snoring, but no sound came from Selby. Otis suspected that he was as watchful as he was himself, probably still cradling the pistol in his hand. Of course Otis was also armed — but the only ammunition he had were the three shots left in the chamber, whereas Selby had a whole beltful of shells. Despite his misgivings, he snatched an hour or so's sleep.

They were on the move long before dawn, crossing a series of defiles and hills spotted with sage and lush grass. Eventually they reached a wide belt of ponderosa forest. When they had passed through this, they found themselves in an upward sloping meadow and gazed at the rocky crags ahead of them. It was from these crags that a smoke signal suddenly rose — white, spherical puffs showing against the searing blue of the sky. These were cut off for half a minute, then repeated.

All three convicts had drawn up. It was Willoughby who broke their silence. 'I guess that means them redbellies know we're here.'

'Maybe,' Selby grunted, 'maybe not. We can't read their sign, so there's no point in reachin' conclusions.'

'Just means we've got to be extra careful from now on,' Otis remarked.

In total agreement they pressed on, climbing steadily, keeping within concealing forest wherever possible, avoiding open ground. When they pulled up again to listen, Willoughby remarked how the birds had gone silent. The entire land seemed to be brooding, as if holding its breath as it awaited something to happen. The three men sensed it, went warily forward. But all the caution in the world couldn't have saved them when they were eventually obliged to leave the cedar forest and cross open meadow.

Without warning, eight mounted Sioux rode over a crest and reined in their ponies no more than fifty yards away, blocking the direction the three convicts would have taken. Stunned by the sudden threat, Otis felt as if the ground was opening up to engulf them. Nonetheless, he snatched the Navy Colt from his waistband. His two companions had also frozen in the knee-high grass. Selby had his pistol raised.

'Jesus!' Willoughby croaked, his inane grin belying the fear that widened his eyes. 'We'll never hold 'em off!'

The Indians starting shouting, wheeling their suddenly prancing mounts. Otis was conscious of a pulse drumming in his temple. He watched with a mixture of fear and morbid fascination, seeing how the Indians raised their lances and buffalo-hide shields in taunting gestures, how each shield was ornamented with feathers and animal tails.

But one warrior, astride a big black horse and wearing a feathered bonnet, did not have a shield or lance. Instead he had a rifle; he cradled it into his shoulder, squinted through the sights and squeezed the trigger. For an Indian, his aim was remarkable. The ball struck Otis in the head, jerking him backwards, splashing his blood across Selby and Willoughby. Otis lay on his back, unmoving, his sightless face turned heavenward, his ears now deaf to the bedlam of savage whooping.

Slamming moccasined heels into the ribs of their ponies, the Indians charged towards the two surviving white men.

2

'Grab the gun!' Selby yelled. Willoughby needed no second bidding. Desperately, he clawed aside the grass to snatch up the Colt that had spun from Otis's grasp. The war whoops of the Indians flooded around them, a deluge of terror. Selby ran for the trees. Willoughby attempted to follow but caught his toe in the grass and went down. He forced himself up to find an Indian almost upon him, the breath of the heaving, wild-eyed mount burning him. Willoughby pointed the pistol, pressed the trigger — but the hammer clicked on an empty chamber. The Indian, hauling back on his reins, swung at Willoughby with his tomahawk, but he missed and for a startling moment the two men glared into each other's eyes. Suddenly a look of horror settled over the Indian's face and he jerked his mount to the side and heeled away.

Gaining brief respite, Willoughby staggered, crouched double, to the cedars. Selby had swung round to kneel and aim his own pistol as Willoughby flung himself down alongside him. Simultaneously, an arrow thumped into a tree-trunk scant feet away, discharged from the back of a galloping mount.

Fanning the hammer, Selby unleashed three shots at an oncoming warrior, grunting with satisfaction as the man threw up his arms and tumbled backwards from his pony, his war-bonnet trailing behind him. Willoughby spun the chamber of his Colt and fired three times, then he realized that his ammunition was exhausted. But Selby was still blasting off, bringing a pony crashing down, spilling its rider into the path of those who followed. The whole charge had come to a milling halt. Even so, sheer force of numbers, sheer renewed momentum, would overwhelm them if the Indians resumed their advance.

Both men scrambled to their feet and fled into the deeper forest, tripping and clawing their way through the undergrowth, running for their lives. As they went, Selby reloaded his weapon. For a good fifteen minutes they rushed on, then, winded, they stopped to listen. Amazingly, the forest about them revealed nothing but its natural sounds. It was almost as if the attack had been an awesome dream.

'My God,' Willoughby panted. 'D'you reckon they've given up on us?'

Selby emitted a grim laugh. 'Hogs might fly. If they catch us, Otis is the lucky one. At least he's dead and gawn.'

'Well,' Willoughby went on, 'if they're trailin' us, they're bein' mighty quiet.'

'Maybe you scared 'em off with that crazy grin of yours. They probably thought you were mad. Injuns always avoid the insane.'

Willoughby nodded. It was not the first time his disfigurement had served him well.

Selby glanced about uneasily. 'On the

other hand, maybe they've circled this wood and are waitin' for us on the far side.' He thumbed a half-dozen shells from his belt and passed them to his companion. 'Guess you'll need these — but you'd best save one for yourself if they catch us.'

Willoughby's grin remained unrelenting. 'We been in tight scrapes before, Will. We ain't finished yet.' He refilled the chamber of his pistol. 'You got any plan?'

'Figure we best stay here for a while. Wait till it gets dark, then, if we've still got our scalps, we'll press on the way we was headed. We can't let those redbellies stop us from reachin' the cash.'

Both men now withdrew into the cover of a thicket and sprawled down watchfully, their hammering senses gradually reverting to normality. The cedars emitted a heady aroma that was strangely stupefying. After a while Willoughby said, 'That Indian you brought down, the one in that war-bonnet. Maybe he was a chief and that's why they've held back.'

'Could be,' Selby agreed. 'In that case, they'll either be crazy for revenge . . . or they'll be lickin' their wounds and cryin' their eyes out.'

Concealed in the thicket, they remained vigilant through the long afternoon. The only sounds they heard came from the birds and the relentless buzz of insects. As dusk at last descended, they had not been further molested or heard any sign of their enemies. Eventually, with starlight sifting down through the overlapping branches, Selby decided they should make a move. He had no intention of leaving the Black Hills; his ambition, and Willoughby's, to reach the loot was as strong as ever. This being so, they retreated cautiously through the woods, covering the ground over which they had fled earlier in the day. Indians had a reputation of not fighting at night for fear of disturbing the spirits. With luck, they might have made camp elsewhere and their thoughts had turned to other things.

At last the two men reached the location where the original skirmish had occurred — and exactly where it had fallen, they spotted Otis's body spread-eagled beneath the moon. 'Wonder if the devils have lifted his scalp,' Willoughby murmured.

Glancing around to ensure that all was quiet, they approached the body and Selby peered close. 'Scalp's still in place,' he grunted.

Willoughby nodded. He'd liked Otis. He felt bad about what had happened. But now he made a startling discovery. 'He ain't dead, Will. Look, his chest is movin'.'

Selby mouthed an obscenity and gazed at what he'd thought was a corpse. After a second, he said, 'You're right. One thing's for sure: he ain't goin' to last much longer. There's nothin' we can do for him.'

'We can dig his grave so's it's ready,' Willoughby said. 'That's the least we can do. No point in leavin' him for all and sundry to see.'

Selby nodded grudgingly.

They found some wood, and close in against the trees they started to scrape a trench into the soft soil. They worked silently, frequently pausing to scan the moonlit terrain for indication of their enemies, but none came and eventually the trench was large enough to take the body. They checked Otis again. His breathing was scarcely noticeable.

'He'll be gone soon,' Selby said. 'Let's rest him in the grave. That'll save time.'

So they struggled with Otis's dead-weight, lowered him into the hole. 'We won't fill it in yet,' Willoughby said. 'We can't bury him alive.'

Selby shrugged his shoulders impatiently but said nothing.

Then they both heard a sound that froze their guts . . . the snorting of a distant horse carried on the night breeze. 'Wait here,' Selby whispered, and he crawled off through the grass. Fifteen minutes later he was back.

'Injuns,' he growled. 'They're camped over the hill.'

'What can we do?' Willoughby asked.

'Keep quiet, and pray they don't get wind of us. We best get away from here while it's dark.'

'That's if Otis is dead. We can't leave him.'

Willoughby took another long look into the grave, then he said, 'I reckon he's a gonna.' They both listened for his breathing. They heard nothing.

'Let's fill in the grave,' Selby said. They started to scrape earth into the hole — but then Otis moaned.

'Shit!' Selby exclaimed. 'I wish he'd get his dyin' done with.' They hunkered on the lip of the grave, their teeth chattering. It was ghostly there, waiting while a man hovered between this world and the next.

At last Selby said, 'There's no point in lingerin'.'

'We can't leave him,' Willoughby repeated.

'Yeah we can,' Selby said. 'You're too

29

soft. Let's fill the earth in and be done with it.'

'Will . . . we should wait till he stops breathin'.'

'Not me,' Selby snorted. 'I'm gettin' out. You can please yourself.'

The two men glanced at each other. Willoughby shook his head. 'Can't do it,' he grunted.

'It's your choice, Grinner. My choice is to get away from here while I've got the chance.' He nodded in a curt farewell, then he rose to his feet and moved off.

Willoughby hesitated. Maybe he was being foolish. Again he listened for Otis's breathing. At first he thought he heard nothing — but as he started to scrape earth into the trench, the faintest sibilance of breath caught his ear. 'Damn you, Otis,' he muttered.

His feelings shifted. Selby was right, same as he generally was. They had done all they could for Otis. They had dug him a grave . . . they had laid him in it . . . all he had to do was die.

Ten minutes later Willoughby followed after his companion. Selby had hauled up in the trees, suspecting that Willoughby would see sense. He'd known him a long time, knew the way his brain functioned.

'You filled the grave in?' he asked.

Willoughby gave a grim nod. 'Sure I did,' he lied.

3

It was the following day. Otis, having recovered consciousness, had crawled out of his grave. He waved a cloud of mosquitoes away. His memory was blank, like a curtain drawn across his past. He shook his head, trying to jar his memory back, but all he got was an intensification of his headache. He inhaled deeply and cajoled his feet into motion. They felt heavy, laced, as they were, in clodhopper boots. He steeled himself against dizziness, his headache. His steps gathered momentum as he stumbled down the slope, crickets leaping away before him. He needed water, food . . . and help.

The sun was directly overhead, fierce as a hawk's eye, and he wished he had a hat. He reached some trees, ponderosa pine, and was thankful for their shade. The scent of resin thickened the air and he felt a grittiness between his teeth. Presently, a rustling of foliage caused him to pull up, fear chilling his sweat. He crouched down, waited.

A bull elk moved into view; shreds of velvet dangled from the antlers which were raised above its head like many-fingered hands. It flexed its nostrils and then sprang off, its rump flashing whitely. It vanished into the forest's obscurity, the sound of its progress fading.

He went on again, his feet sinking into a carpet of pine needles; he had no idea where he was heading but knew that it was easier to go down-slope than up. Ten minutes later; the trees thinned and he emerged on to another meadow. Across it a stream gurgled, widening into a pool before flowing onward through rocks. The water caught the sun's glint, half dazzling him with its myriad of diamonds. The prospect of slaking his thirst drew him into the open, heedless of danger.

Sprawled face down, he guzzled water

and afterwards stripped and submerged his body, gasping yet grateful for its cleansing iciness. He discovered that he was a hairy, stocky man. Supporting himself against a rock, he gazed at his naked image on the pool's surface. The slitted eyes were bloodshot and wild. Turning his head slightly, he saw the reflection of the wound and he winced. He carefully washed away the congealed blood.

This person was a stranger to him. He was not the sort he would choose for acquaintance. Turning away, he dried himself with grass and pulled on the arrowhead suit and boots. He wished he could dump this clothing, but he had nothing else to wear. Refreshed, he forced himself on, his belly growling with hunger.

Near to an oak copse, he spotted some fungi growing in a group. They had high, white caps with pale brown scales. On impluse, he broke the stems and slipped them into his mouth. They were crunchy and not distasteful. Once started, his ravenousness got the better of him. He demolished the whole group before he allowed himself to wonder if they were poisonous. He shrugged the thought away, glad that his hunger was temporarily satisfied. Further on he ate some hazelnuts and green plums.

He pressed forward, gaining his second wind, and hours later a sound buzzed in his ears. It was like the humming of a sawmill. He paused, puzzled, then continued cautiously through the trees. The sound rose to dinning proportions. He reached a clearing and saw the burial scaffold, supported by four poles anchored within cairns of stones. It had not been weathered by time; it must have been recently erected. A sickly sweetness fouled the air.

Flies were responsible for the noise. There were thousands, giant blue-bottles, buzzing in a cloud about the horse's head tied to one of the poles; it was decorated with feathers but every-thing was blackened by swarming insects. The decapitation had been clumsily done. The animal's long tail adorned another pole.

Fanning aside flies, he craned his neck for a better view. Upon the scaffold's platform of crossed boughs, some eight feet from the ground, was a blanket-shrouded bundle — obviously a corpse. No doubt it was an Indian of importance, perhaps a chief, left to dry out before the bones were laid to final rest.

He shuddered; he recalled how close he too had been to death. It had brushed him like a raven's wing. Having no wish to seek companionship from a departed spirit, he was about to press on when a possibility came to him.

He stood beneath the platform in the very spot between head and tail, where the horse's body would have been had it been left whole. He gazed upward through the slatted branches upon which the corpse lay. There was something beside it, something that glinted. Grunting with satisfaction, he

36

found a nearby, low branch and snapped it off. He stripped away the leaves, then returned to the scaffold and probed upward through the slatted boughs with his stick. Patiently, he worked the object sideways until it toppled from the platform and thudded down at his feet. It was a knife. He wondered if it had been used to scalp some poor soul. It was an Indian custom to leave such weapons alongside the dead for their use in the spirit world. He picked it up. It was bone-handled with a long, sharp blade upon which were engraved the words: MADE IN SHEFFIELD.

Gripping his newly acquired weapon, he resumed his journey, trudging through forest and across lower hills. There was something eerie about the terrain. It seemed like an alien world. He lost count of time, but the sun arced across the sky and grew more benign. Meanwhile, his feet had become leaden, his belly was churning, his strength ebbing . . . and then the acridity of smoke caught in his throat. He was standing on an undulating slope. Further down, a lightning-felled oak obscured his view. Crouching, he crept forward. Soon he was peering through the tangle of blackened branches.

His breath died.

Scarcely twenty yards from him, six Indians were hunkered about a fire in the dip of a hollow. Their feathers showed white in the weakening sun; their lank hair hung shoulder-long and straight. Black markings were streaked across their bodies. They were feeding, gnawing at bones. Beyond them a number of ponies grazed in a meadow.

His befuddled brain could recall no reason why he should fear these savages; even so, he shrank to the ground behind the fallen tree, cursing its inadequate cover. His initial panic receded, then, gradually, he started to breathe again, praying that he had not already sent out some sound which would bring them to investigate. Wounded and weak, he would prove easy pickings if they chose to take his scalp. He wondered if it was they who had wounded him. If so, why hadn't they finished him off? Another likelihood struck him. The black-daubed Indians were clearly in mourning. The man left upon the scaffold had perhaps been a respected fellow-warrior. Perhaps they were eager to avenge his death.

And perhaps he, himself, had killed him. He had no way of telling. Now, head down and pressed against the earth, his view of the Indians was obscured, but he could hear them clearly enough . . . the guttural grunt of voices, their belching, the crackle of the campfire. Thoughts of the meat they'd been chewing, the bones they'd been sucking, made him salivate. He was still hungry despite the fungi, hazelnuts and plums.

He glanced at the sky. The sun was well into its westward drift, shadowing the hills and bringing a chill to the twilight air. From the trees whip-poor-wills cried plaintively, welcoming the dusk.

His mind dwelt on the horses grazing in the meadow. If he had a mount, his chances of reaching civilization would increase. What he would do then was open to conjecture.

He knew that while any light remained, he was trapped in his present hiding place. It was surprising that the Indians' nature-honed senses had not already detected his presence. Perhaps they were so steeped in mourning, so craving for revenge, that they had become careless. But any shifting of his position, backward or forward, was sure to alert them. And there was something else troubling him: his belly was full of pain.

He tensed as he heard a rustling in the grass — moccasins; one of the Indians was coming towards him. Sweat beaded out on his face. He was convinced he was about to be discovered. He gripped the knife, braced himself for a sudden strike, followed by a desperate run for his life, but then the footsteps stopped and there sounded the splash of water striking the opposite side of his tree trunk. The spattering continued, seemingly unending. How could any man pee for so long! Eventually it ceased, the Indian hawked and spat, stood for a moment breathing in the cool, evening air, and finally turned to walk back to the campfire.

As relief cut through him, Otis wondered if this party might travel on before nightfall. He waited, hearing little sound from the direction of the camp. He lay motionless, trying to ignore the buzz of mosquitoes, feeling the earth's dampness and the prickle of small insects exploring and biting him. Presently a mouse scurried across only inches from his nose. When darkness deepened, he risked a glance out from his cover. The moon had not yet come, but the dying fire emitted a faint glimmer, just sufficient to reveal the recumbent figures about it. He wondered if they had posted a guard.

He considered his options. Certainly, he could creep away unseen, but his

progress would be meandering and slow
— and they might pick up his trail. He
would be better served if he was astride
a fleet pony. But it would not be easy.
Fear, weariness and pain plagued him.
He closed his eyes, dozed and awoke
with a start, cursing his carelessness. He
could so easily have been discovered
and killed while he slept. He had no
idea how much time had elapsed,
although the moon was now high.

Again he peered from behind his
cover, satisfying himself that the Indians
at the campfire were slumbering. He
heard a shuffling movement from
beyond, and realized that it came from
the ponies in the meadow. The prospect
of a guard made him uneasy. It was a
chance he had to take. At least he had
the knife.

Striving to suppress any sound, he
slowly worked clear of the fallen tree,
backing up the slope a good twenty
yards before pausing to listen. He
started anxiously as a coyote lifted its
cry into the night — three sharp barks

followed by a sustained high-pitched howl. It sounded so close. He waited awhile, then, crouching low, he started to circle the camp. There was no breeze; even so he knew that the ponies might get scent of him and set up a nervous racket.

It took him a good hour to reach the spot on the far side that he wanted, opposite his original hiding place. The ponies were now directly between him and the last glimmer of the fire. He rested, gathering his courage and what remained of his strength. He wished the cloud would obscure the moon but it did not. At last he made his move, his heart thudding like a trip-hammer.

He was twenty feet from the shadowy hulks of the ponies when he heard their nervous stomping — and then their high-pitched whinnying shattered his last vestige of surprise. They were panicking, their rolling eyes showing white in the gloom. He heard alarmed shouting from the Indians as they jumped up.

He sprang amongst the beasts, knowing that his enemies would be scurrying to investigate. His hand closed over a rope hobbling the forelegs of the nearest pony and he hung on to it, left-handed, amid prancing hooves. He slashed at it with the knife, missed, tried again. This time the honed blade severed the threads but sliced his fingers in the process, flooding them with blood. Reaching up, he seized the animal's mane, the knife slipping from his hand. There was no time to recover it. With strength borne of desperation, he leaped upwards, clinging right-sided like an Indian as he forced his leg over the animal's back. The beast was off immediately, fear stampeding it through the trees, bucking this way and that in a vain effort to dislodge its unwelcome burden.

He hugged on, arms encircling the neck, impervious to the bruising jolt as his teeth clamped the mane, the scrape of low branches raking him. Riding bareback, without bridle or halter, he had no alternative but to go wherever the pony carried him — and hope that its hooves would outdistance any pursuers.

Fungi-instilled pain was scything through his guts, but he ignored it. There was something more urgent troubling him. Something he had foolishly over-looked — namely that his free-galloping mount would follow its natural instincts and head for home.

Home being an Indian village.

4

Rachel emptied the bucket of kitchen scraps into the hog-pen, murmuring tender words to the snorting animals. She loved them and grieved deeply when her pa took the knife to one, feeling that she had lost a true friend. In return, her pa and brother Jacob would laugh scornfully, saying that she was too soft, like her mother had been. She tried to console herself with the belief that until the day their throats were slit, the hogs had a good life. At least they could do what they pleased, following their natural instincts without having religion quoted at them every second of the day.

Rachel was eighteen, a well-proportioned girl with a wide mouth and large dew-drop eyes which were the colour of blueberries. Right now she lingered at the hog-pen, glad to be away from the kitchen chores for a moment.

'Where's that girl!' she heard her father shout from the cabin. 'She gets lazier by the minute.'

Holy Jack Surestep had worked their smallholding in the shadow of the Black Hills for the past fifteen years, allowing only his son Jacob to accompany him to Horn Ridge Springs, the small township twenty miles south, for provisions. His wife and daughter never left the immediate vicinity of the neighbourless smallholding, for Holy Jack knew the corruption that the outsiders could bring to folks, particularly women. He had seen how females could be distracted from their natural duties and he had striven to prevent his own kind from straying from the path of righteousness. He had not even allowed Rachel to attend the schoolhouse, insisting that her mother provide the learning. What had been forthcoming had been liberally seasoned with resentment against the man who made their lives such pious misery.

Jack was constantly in a bad and

vicious humour, caused to a large extent by the pain he suffered with his decaying teeth and gums that glowed like hot coals. He refused adamantly to have his teeth pulled, having the strange notion that bearing this awful discomfort gave him the right to act mean. After all, God had given him the teeth in the first place.

Throughout the years, the Surestep family had been held in strange awe by the Sioux Indians who believed that Holy Jack was in direct communication with the spirits in the skies. Once, when the homestead had been raided by marauding Kiowa, the Sioux had even stepped in to drive them away. Holy Jack had registered his gratitude with coffee, whiskey and supplies — and later on with guns.

But the hard and lonely life had taken its toll. Emma Surestep, who had been a beautiful woman before being worn down by the pitiful life, had been smitten with the ague. Despite Holy Jack rubbing her skin nigh raw with a salve of turpentine and goose grease, she passed away within a week, leaving her daughter to carry the burden of caring for two menfolk.

Now, as Rachel returned to the cabin, smoothing back her dark hair, she passed the spot marked with a cross and knew, that even in death, her mother had been unable to escape this awful place. To the side, was another grave, unmarked and grown over. Her father had forbidden her to think about it or even glance at it — but she would always remember the man who was buried there.

A month back, just after Holy Jack had killed their old dog Elijah in a fit of pique, Rachel had told herself that she could stand life here no longer. Secretly, she had drawn a few meagre possessions together and packed them in a saddle-bag; then, seeing her chance, she had saddled Apple, her Appaloosa pony, and ridden out, intent on running away. But Holy Jack and Jacob had chased her and, within five miles, had caught her.

Retribution had been swift. Believing that he was fulfilling the wrath of the Lord, her father had beaten her with a strap. Even now, the cuts and bruises pained her. Her father's final act of punishment had fanned the burning hatred in her heart: it was like a blast of breath on a branding iron. To ensure she made no further attempts at escape, Holy Jack had traded off her pony Apple and forbidden her to step outside the fenced pastures of the smallholding. But he didn't know that she had built up a steady supply of food — tins of bacon, lard, hardtack, pemmican; as well as a small number of utensils and other necessaries which she had hidden in an outhouse in readiness for her next bid for freedom.

Today, there were matters, apart from his recalcitrant daughter, annoying Holy Jack. As Rachel entered the cabin's untidy living-room, the old man was seated at the table, peering at the newspaper spread before him.

Standing alongside him was his

sixteen-year-old son, a lesser image of the father. Jacob, cursed by a stammer, said, 'You s-say an army expedition is c-comin' into the hills, Pa?'

Holy Jack frowned, running his gnarled finger down the newspaper column. 'Says that General George A. Custer's Seventh Cavalry is carryin' out a reconnaissance of the Black Hills, maybe set up a military post or two.' He shook his head with disgust. 'That's contrary to Red Cloud's treaty of '68. The Black Hills was given to the Sioux for ever. They won't take kindly to no white folks intrudin' into that country. It'll bring trouble; you mark my words.'

Suddenly there was a crash. Rachel had dropped a plate, smashing it into fragments on the hard-mud floor. Both males swung round to see the girl gazing through the doorway. Before Holy Jack could express his fury at the breaking of valuable crockery, Rachel cried out, 'Rider comin' in!' Then, with astonishment, she added, 'He's ridin' Apple!'

51

Holy Jack was on his feet directly, grabbing hold of his rifle.

★ ★ ★

Otis had clung to the Appaloosa's back through the remaining hours of darkness, fearful that the Indians would give chase. His body ached from the battering it had taken, his head and guts were churning with pain, despite the fact that he had vomited the unwholesome fungi from his belly. His memory still told him nothing of events prior to the time when he had dragged himself from his grave. Now, as the day's light grew stronger, clearing away the dawn mists, his suspicions reached fruition — at least partially. Right enough, his mount had carried him out of the hills to its natural home. However, this was not an Indian village as he had feared.

His tired gaze took in the fenced pastures where a number of cows and horses grazed. He saw the potato and corn crops, the rambling hog and chicken pens, an empty water-trough, a woodpile, a cross marking a grave. Nestled in the streamside meadow, a decrepit cabin stood, its cedar-log walls lacking windows but showing numerous rifle-ports. Smoke lifted from the abode's chimney. He glanced around, at first noticing no other sign of life. Too exhausted to take precautions, he slid stiffly from his mount. Once on the ground, he swayed, almost fell, but somehow retained his balance.

It was then that Holy Jack's order scythed through the silence. 'Stay where you are, mister!'

Instinctively, Otis raised his hands, then focused his gaze. The owner of the voice was a bearded old man in a floppy, wide-brimmed hat, standing in the shadow of the cabin's stoop. He was wizened and as skinny as a stovepipe. He reminded Otis of a muskrat. His horny hands were gripping a twin-barrelled, sawn-off Remington.

Holy Jack jerked his gun menacingly. 'How come you got that pony?'

Otis glanced back at the Appaloosa which was now grazing contentedly on the pasture. 'Borrowed it from an Indian.'

Holy Jack snorted with disbelief. 'Stole it, most likely. I traded that beast to the Sioux three weeks back. Indians don't appreciate horse-theft any more than whites. You'll probably bring a war-party down on us.'

Otis did not argue.

'Who are you?' the old man demanded, then, noting his visitor's soiled prison-garb, he provided his own answer. 'I know who you are.' And now there was an undercurrent of excitement in his words. 'Sheriff Rainbird was talkin' about escaped prisoners when I was in town yesterday. Talked about a bounty that's being offered for their capture, dead or alive.'

'Bounty?' Otis said vaguely, but there were more important matters on his mind. 'Guess it's no good asking you for help, then?'

Holy Jack licked his lips. 'Well, boy, I

54

won't turn you over if you make it worth my while. I been on my knees every night, prayin' to the Lord for you to come.' Slyly he added, 'I heard talk of stolen cash.'

'Cash?' Otis raised his eyebrows. He wished he could brush aside the barrier that concealed his past.

The old man unleashed a laugh. 'Don't you play ignorant with me. I know all about the pay-roll raid those years back; how that fortune was hidden up some place and never recovered. Sheriff Rainbird told me how three fellas escaped when they was being transferred to Canby City, how they ran off across the river. Two of those sinners were them that thieved the cash, hid it before they got caught.'

Otis felt no recollection; it was as if the story related to complete strangers. 'And the third man?' he queried.

Holy Jack's face sparked with impatience. 'Get into the cabin fast, mister. Ain't no point in standin' out here, tellin' you what you already know. Them

Indians may ride over the hill any minute. I've always been friendly with the red varmints, but something like this could stir them up. Keep your hands raised and don't figure on any tricks. We've got some hard talkin' to do.'

Otis looked at the rambling old cabin, seeing how its timbers were rotting and its roof was sprouting with growth, including wild flowers.

Holy Jack kept his gun levelled, and there was a meanness about the way his finger curled around the unguarded trigger that convinced Otis on the futility of argument. This man was crazy; it showed in his squinting eyes.

Otis wondered if his own eyes were playing tricks. It seemed he was seeing double. A figure identical to the old man's had appeared on the cabin's stoop — the same stooped shoulders, floppy hat, scruffy clothing. But as they got closer, he could see that the pointed, muskrat features belonged to a younger fellow — maybe in his teens.

'Get a rope, Jacob,' Holy Jack

ordered. 'We want this fella tied up real tight.'

'Y-yes, Pa,' the boy stuttered, moving away.

'I'm not planning to run off,' Otis protested. 'I guess I done enough running for the present.'

Holy Jack glared at him. 'Don't cross me, boy. I'm awful dangerous when I'm crossed!'

A moment later, Otis was standing in the cabin's untidy living-room, an odour of stale bodies and decay filling the air, all backed by a lingering taint of turpentine. As his vision adjusted to the dim interior, he saw how the place was crammed with cheap religious ornaments. Several sets of antlers and a moth-eaten, spreadeagled bearskin decorated the walls. A black stove stood in the corner, flame showing through its cracks, its pipe going out through the roof. At the back, several more rooms and a passage-way led off.

The old man kept the Remington pointed while his son returned and fastened Otis's hands behind his back; then they bound his ankles together. Without warning, Holy Jack gave him a cruel shove in the chest. Otis toppled down on to the floor, landing heavily, the old man's laugh in his ears. When this subsided, Holy Jack wiped his spittled lips with the back of his hand. 'Which of them sinners is you?' he asked, angling his head to catch the answer.

Otis was sprawled face down with the taste of blood in his mouth. 'I don't know who I am.'

A boot slammed into his side, making him grunt with pain. 'I ain't playin' games, mister!' Holy Jack grunted. 'Like I said, I can maybe do business with you if you've got a heap of cash hidden up some place. That's why I been prayin' for you to come. But if you're that third fella, that Otis Lockhart, you're real trash and you'll get what you deserve. I'll not have you lustin' for my daughter. I'll take the knife to you, same as I do my hogs. Only I won't be cutting your throat, I'll be slicing off your . . . '

'Pa!'

Otis raised his head and saw the girl.

She was wearing a soiled blue dress of calico, but this accentuated rather than concealed her maturing womanliness. She was barefoot.

'Pa,' she repeated in a quieter voice, 'there's an awful wound on his head; looks as if a bullet has grooved along his skull. It's bleedin'. Can I bandage it?'

Holy Jack cursed, but after a second he nodded. 'Bandage him, Rachel. Rub some soot into the wound. That'll stop the blood. We don't want him dying on us, not until we find out who he is and what he knows. Don't talk to him or anythin'. Don't do nothin' 'cept bandage him.'

Otis was trussed up like a hapless fowl, yet the presence of the girl had somehow quickened his pulse. Rachel fetched some bandage, a handful of soot and a bowl of water.

'Turn over, mister . . . please.' Her request was surprisingly respectful.

Otis obliged by clumsily rolling himself onto his back, then the girl went to work, bathing his head, applying the soot, her hands showing considerable tenderness. As she fastened the bandage, she knelt so close that her breasts touched him. Her lips were pursed and she was making a soothing sound. There was about her a womanly smell that aroused a strange sensation inside him. How could a monstrous old man like Holy Jack have such an angelic daughter? Maybe he wasn't her true father.

'You b-better hurry up,' her brother Jacob was stammering, 'else P-Pa will g-get angry again.'

Otis figured the old man had gone outside so he risked a question. 'What's this about your Pa praying for me to come here?'

Holy Jack was near enough to hear him. He stamped in and kicked Otis in the ribs, knocking his daughter's bowl of water over in the process.

As Otis lay groaning, the old man was

screaming, 'Ain't nobody's business why I pray, 'cept mine and the Lord's. You understand that, mister, or you'll feel my knife. Nobody 'll be any the wiser!'

Otis shuddered. He was utterly at his mercy.

Suddenly they all heard voices coming from outside. Holy Jack grunted to Jacob to help him, and together they grasped Otis and dragged him across the floor to the back of the room. Seconds later he'd been dropped into a deep hole, a root-cellar, with a trap-door bolted above his head. He was in darkness, with the smell of decaying vegetables almost gassing him. My God, he thought, why did I have to come to this crazy hell on earth?

Holy Jack had stepped outside to meet the posse of eight riders who were reining in their horses in front of the cabin. Leading them was Fred Rainbird, Sheriff of Horn Ridge Springs. He was a sturdy, square-built man wearing a heavily beaded buckskin vest and a crimson bandanna. There was a deep scar on his left cheek. He kept widening his nostrils, like a hunter sniffing for spoor. 'Howdy, Mr Surestep,' he nodded. 'We come to enquire if you've caught sight of them escaped convicts?'

The old man gave his head a shake. 'I ain't seen a livin' soul around these parts for weeks . . . but me and my children'll keep our eyes skinned, and if we do spy them devils, we'll let you know.'

'They're real dangerous, Holy Jack. Two of 'em were leaders of the gang that lifted the government pay-roll down at Sand Springs. They hid the stuff before they got caught — a real fortune, for sure. But it's the third fella you gotta watch for, that Otis Lockhart.'

'Yeah,' Holy Jack said. 'I heard he murdered three women — raped and murdered 'em. Treated 'em real bad. He's sick for sure.'

'He cut 'em up into bits, worse'n any Indian. He scattered them bits across the prairie. Why he didn't get the rope, God only knows. Judge must've gone soft. Keep a tight watch on your daughter. Ain't no tellin' what he'll try now he's on the loose again. Next time he gets caught, he won't get things so easy.'

'I hear a bounty's been offered for all three men?' Holy Jack said.

'Sure . . . dead or alive. Anyway, keep a watch out. If they show up, send your son hell for leather to let us know.' He unbuckled his saddle-bag, reached inside and drew out a sheaf of papers. 'Here, pin these Wanted notices up in your cabin. They'll remind you. We'll catch them sons of bitches one way or the other. That's for certain.'

Holy Jack took the notices. 'We'll keep a watch out, Sheriff.'

He stood, observing the posse trail off over the ridge, the dust gradually settling in their wake.

Meanwhile, Otis was sprawled on the earth floor of the cellar. He was in darkness. He realized something was crawling over his face; he shook it off. His new prison was alive with cockroaches. It was also very small. He was sick of being shoved into holes. From what he'd been told, he'd pieced together some idea of his past and it was far from reassuring. Maybe it would be better if everything remained a blank.

Presently the trap-door was opened and the old man lowered himself down beside him. He seemed mighty pleased about something. 'We done you a big favour,' he said. 'The sheriff is out huntin' for you, but we sent him away. I figure he can catch the other two fellas first. Now, you just tell me where you got that cash hid.'

'I don't know,' Otis groaned.

'There's only one of the three convicts that wouldn't know where the loot is hid, and that's Otis Lockhart. Are you tellin' me you're a filthy, murderin' rapist? Because if you are' — Holy Jack drove his hand across Otis's face, his sharp ring snagging his cheek — 'the Lord will condemn your soul to purgatory!'

There was light coming through from the open trap-door, and Otis could see the old man's face . . . the bulging eyes; the lips drawn snarlingly back from yellow teeth and tumid gums; and it seemed to Otis that this man was far more dangerous than all the Indians of the Sioux Nation put together.

At last Holy Jack got his emotions under control. 'Tell me where the cash is,' he repeated, 'otherwise, I won't have no option but to give you the punishment you deserve.'

Otis shook his head in misery. 'Can't you undo these ropes? I won't run away.'

The old man laughed scornfully. 'I know what's in your dirty mind, mister. I recognized the lust in your eyes when you spied Rachel. I ain't unleashin' your hands so you can maul her sweet body. I'll give you until tomorrow to recall where the cash is hid. If you ain't remembered, you'll face the consequences.'

He reached up and hauled himself

out of the cellar, bolts slammed across the trap-door and Otis was in darkness again.

He lay for hours, tormented by pain, pestered by the relentless scurryings of cockroaches. He was exasperated by the blankness in his mind, yet frightened that if his memory returned, it would tell him the most awful things. Who the hell am I? Am I really that Otis Lockhart — rapist and murderer? Oh God!

Much later, the trap-door was opened. This time it was Jacob who peered down at him. 'Pa said I was to t-take you out to the privy, that I was to shoot you if you t-tried to escape.'

Otis nodded, thankful that he might at last be allowed to stretch his painful limbs. Jacob watched him relentlessly, his finger touching the trigger of the Remington. With his free hand he slackened the ropes about Otis's ankles. Otis groaned with the sudden wave of renewed cramp and worked his legs, anxious to stimulate the blood.

He hobbled after Jacob, not seeing either the old man or Rachel as he passed through the cabin to the outside privy. On return, Jacob again forced him into the cellar and tightened the rope about his ankles, after which he fetched some corn-pudding, a wrinkled apple and a jug of water. He was taking no chances. He did not loosen Otis's hands, but undertook the feeding and watering of the prisoner himself.

As Otis swallowed the last of the pudding, Jacob said, 'I b-been looking at them W-Wanted notices. It says that murderin' r-rapist Otis Lockhart can easily be recognized 'cos he's got a reddish beard and a kink in his nose where it was once broke.'

Otis inhaled sharply. 'There's a lot of men around with reddish beards and kinks in their noses.' He realized how stupid this sounded. He could no more convince himself than he could anybody else. The awesome knowledge took hold of his mind. I am Otis Lockhart; there can be no doubt.

Jacob didn't respond.

'Has your pa seen those notices?' Otis asked.

'He ain't g-got round to readin' them y-yet, but he sure w-will soon. Once he d-does, he'll get all stirred up . . . like he did b-before.'

'Before?' Otis queried.

Jacob shrugged his thin shoulders. 'Ain't for me t-to t-tell you, Mr Lockhart. Pa'll t-tell you hisself, if he wants you to know.' With that he started to climb from the cellar, but Otis called to him in desperation. 'These ropes . . . they're so tight. They're stopping my blood flowing. Can't you slacken them a bit?'

'Pa said to t-tie you real t-tight.'

'But . . . '

Jacob turned away and lowered the trap-door.

Otis, again in Stygian gloom, collapsed back on to the filthy, insect-seething floor of his prison. He groaned with wretchedness. Earlier he had tried to persuade himself that he

68

could never have committed those terrible crimes . . . but now a new and deepening awareness had taken hold of him. An awareness that the mere nearness of Rachel, with her young body, aroused in him a craven desire. And this despite his weakened, helpless state. Perhaps Holy Jack had been right to suspect him of possessing abnormal lusts . . .

Otis had no way of telling how much time elapsed. Mosquitoes had found their way into the cellar. His entire body tormented him; he just concentrated on drawing the foul air into his lungs, holding it, then exhaling. Presently he lapsed into a stupor. When he awoke he guessed it was much later. Must be night time. No sounds came from the cabin above; the family must have bedded down. Soon, utter despair and weakness had him dozing . . . but then suddenly he was roused. The subdued creak of the trap-door warned him that he was no longer alone. He tensed against his bonds. Simultaneously he heard the soft pant of the girl's breathing and his senses quickened.

'I need to talk with you,' Rachel whispered, as she lowered herself down beside him. They were in complete darkness still. 'We got to be quiet. Pa would go crazy if he knew I was here. He's swore no man should touch me, that the Lord has some special task for me. That's why that awful thing happened the last time. Mister, tell me somethin'. You ain't that fella who treats women rough are you, that Otis Lockhart?' She hesitated, waiting for his response, then she said, 'But I guess it don't make no difference, seeing as you're tied up.'

'Rachel, these ropes are so tight. Slacken them off a bit. I promise I won't tell your pa.'

She hesitated, then said, 'Oh, well!' and her fingers grappled with the knots and with relief he realized their awful hold was loosened, though not enough for him to get free.

He worked his limbs as best he could,

easing painful life back into them. 'I'm truly grateful,' he murmured, and then he recalled her earlier words. 'You mentioned a last time; what happened that last time?'

She sighed impatiently. 'If I tell you, mister, for God's sake you won't let on, will you?'

'I won't,' he said.

She took a deep breath, then started. 'It was after that cash robbery, after them outlaws hid the loot. One of them . . . his name was Charlie Casement . . . got separated from the others, turned up here like you did. He promised he'd tell Pa where the cash was hid, if Pa would help him escape. Pa wasn't taking any chances. He kept Charlie tied up, just like you are. Charlie and me got to know each other. He was real nice. But Pa caught us together, like you and I are now, and he went crazy, said Charlie and me were up to sinful, filthy deeds.' She paused having somehow got choked up with emotion, but Otis felt a driving urge to learn more.

'Had you committed sins, Rachel?'

She had recovered herself slightly. 'I've heard that what some men and women do together is sinful, something they call fornication. But I could never have done anything like that because I don't know how. Pa always told me that I would never have the need to know because I must remain pure . . . '.

He gasped disbelievingly as she went on. 'After Pa caught us together, he forgot all about the cash, grabbed Charlie by the throat and choked him to death. It was terrible . . . then he got hold of me and thrashed me till I was raw. Afterwards, he buried Charlie near Ma's grave. Never put no cross on it though. Ever since then, he's cursed himself for what he did, for not gettin' the whereabouts of the cash out of Charlie before he killed him. He kept prayin' that one day somebody else from the gang would arrive here and he'd have a second chance. That's why he's so glad you've come.'

'He strangled this man while he was bound like me?' Otis gasped.

'Keep your voice down,' she whispered urgently. 'Say, if you're not Otis Lockhart, what's your true name?'

It seemed she hadn't read those Wanted notices, not yet.

'I can't remember,' Otis said. 'Bullet across my head must've robbed me of my memory.'

She waited a moment as if reaching some conclusion. 'Well, I shall call you Johnny . . . Johnny No Name.' He felt her hand touch his face, then she whispered, 'Will you let me kiss you, Johnny No Name?'

'If that's what you want.'

'Oh yes. That's what I want right enough.' Her lips touched his cheek, lingered and then with her fingers she turned his head to draw his mouth to hers, kissing him as if he was the last man in the world. He was tingling all over. It was incredible that this girl could stir him despite his harrowing circumstances. But suddenly his mind was drifting to the old man, to the murder he had committed — and, as if in confirmation of Otis's worst fears, a footstep sounded from above and light flooded down into the cellar.

He felt a shocked spasm pass through the girl as she drew back. 'Oh no!' she groaned.

'You sure are a wi-wicked girl!'

Otis glanced at Rachel in the flickering candle-light. Anger had got to her, making her fine, young breasts heave with emotion.

'Jacob,' she seethed, 'why can't you mind your own business!'

Otis realized that it was Holy Jack's stammering son who had disturbed them. He was holding a candle and peering down. 'Rachel!' he was saying, 'G-get back to b-bed before Pa wakes up!' Jacob was trying to keep his voice hushed, but anxiousness had forced a harsh edge on to it.

'I hate Pa,' Rachel hissed, easing herself back from Otis. 'I hate him! I hate him!'

With a sudden lithe movement she reached up and pulled herself out of the cellar. She glanced back at Otis, the glisten of tears showing in her eyes. Almost inaudibly she whispered, 'Johnny . . . Johnny No Name.' A moment later she and her brother were gone, the trap-door closed and the bolt slipped quietly back in place. Feet scudded across the boards; brief, angry whisperings sounded — and then silence.

5

The Sioux hunting party drifted down from the hills like wolves, the black, mourning paint on their bodies blending into the dark shadows of the forest. They were depleted; there were now six warriors where previously there had been eight. Young Running Elk, had gone on alone in pursuit of the two white men. And, more importantly, their chief Red Bonnet was at rest on his burial scaffold, killed by the *wasicun* intruders. The news would bring grief when they returned to their village on the banks of the Powder River; the fact that Red Bonnet's precious hunting knife had been removed from the scaffold would increase the anguish — an anguish that would be soothed only if revenge had been adequately inflicted on those guilty of the crime.

Iron Shield, who now led the

remaining pack, was dark skinned, his back straight as an arrow. A single eagle feather, worn at the back, decorated his long braids. A choker of bear claws ringed his neck. It was he who had found Red Bonnet's knife after the pony had been stolen at their camp. It had glinted in the moonlight, as if signalling its anger. When he had picked it up from the meadow grass, he had experienced shocked dismay at what had happened. To steal from the burial scaffold was, in Indian eyes, the greatest insult that could be inflicted, the most wicked sacrilege.

In the darkness the thief had got away — but the Indians eventually reasoned out where the pony would take him. This was confirmed when they later discovered some tracks, following them southward out of the hills. Their surmising was proved correct. The pony was going back to Holy Jack's small-holding. It was here they would find the animal, and also, hopefully, the pony-stealer who had moved the knife. He must pay for what he had done. Perhaps they would cut his hands off and pull out his tongue.

Iron Shield was burning with rancour, as were the other warriors. He had never trusted the whites, never expected they would keep their word about staying out of the sacred hills which the Indians called *Paha Sapa*. For generations the Sioux had viewed *Paha Sapa*, which were in reality mountains rather than hills, as 'the heart of everything that is', a place of the gods, a spiritual haven where warriors went to speak with *Wakan Tanka* the great spirit, and await visions. It had been five summers since Chief Red Cloud had put his name to the treaty and later gone to live at the new agency at Fort Laramie. He was a fool to trust the whites. Many Sioux whispered that he had sold himself for a feast of crackers and molasses.

Not all Indians followed Red Cloud's example. Crazy Horse, Sitting Bull and Red Bonnet believed it was better to pitch their villages and hunt buffalo in the Powder River country than eat wormy pork at the agency. And for a time the government had allowed them to remain 'wild', respecting the treaty whereby it had been agreed that the Black Hills, east of the Powder River, would belong to the Indians for all time.

But Iron Shield believed that all *wasicuns* had forked tongues, though he did tolerate Holy Jack whose homestead they now approached. It was just before dawn, with the eastern sky made restless by fingers of pale light. Tendrils of mist rose from the land, muffling the thud of hooves in the spongy soil. As they approached the cabin, a murmur of excitement went through the warriors. They had recognized the stolen Appaloosa grazing in the meadow. The animal was unmistakable with its spotted rump.

The Indians rode directly to the cabin and dismounted. Their manners did not coincide with white manners. The Sioux had no concept of waiting to be invited in.

Holy Jack and Jacob were seated at the table by the light of an oil lamp; Jack had just bitten into a biscuit and nearly hit the roof with the pain his rotten teeth gave him. As he recovered he wondered where Rachel had got to and concluded that she had probably gone to the outhouse; hence the cabin door had been left unbolted.

At that moment Iron Shield and his companions burst in.

Holy Jack sprang to his feet, his chair toppling backwards. He wished he hadn't killed the old dog Elijah; at least it would have yapped out a warning. He also regretted that his gun was across the room. This was not the first time the Indians had come, but Holy Jack had the feeling that now they were motivated by something more than plain sociability and a desire for provisions.

True enough, the Indians barged into the back rooms of the cabin, opening cupboards and tipping furniture over as they searched. Iron Shield had not offered the customary palm-out sign of peace. Instead, he announced, 'We have come for the *wasicun* who stole the pony and moved the knife from Red Bonnet's scaffold.'

'Red Bonnet's scaffold?' Holy Jack exclaimed. 'Is he dead?'

Iron Shield nodded grimly. 'Killed by strangers — men in suits marked with arrows. They too must die. Two are still in the Black Hills. Running Elk has trailed them and will kill them. The other is here. We have come for him.'

Holy Jack's thoughts were racing. If he handed over his prisoner to the Indians, he would never find out where the cash was hidden. On the other hand, the Indians outnumbered him and his son and could easily take what they wanted. Certainly, they could take the pony. Rachel had done nothing virtuous to deserve its return.

'The pony is yours,' he announced. 'You must have it.'

'And the one who stole it?' Iron Shield persisted, jerking his tomahawk suggestively. His companions were crowding around, their faces fierce. One of them had drawn an arrow from his quiver, was fitting it to his bow.

Holy Jack cursed. He had been outwitted. Now he knew that he would be murdered in his own cabin unless he provided what these red heathens wanted. He nodded to Jacob. 'Bring him out of the cellar.'

Jacob stepped across the room, grabbed the handle on the cellar's trap-door and lifted it open. His reaction was startling; he craned his neck to peer down into the small hole, his eyes wide with amazement. 'He ain't h-here, Pa!'

'What the . . . ?' His father scrambled to join him and gaze downward. In the dim light all that was visible on the cellar floor were bits of cut rope, decaying vegetables and scurrying beetles.

Now Holy Jack recalled his daughter's absence, and as the truth seeped into his brain, his face went red, his jowls shook and his wrath uncoiled. He danced about, all horns and rattles, his lips frothing as he screamed profanities, causing even the Indians to step back in alarm.

* * *

The girl's reappearance, those hours earlier, had frightened Otis. *Oh God. the old man will discover us, a voice inside him cried. He'll murder me same way as he did Charlie Casement . . . and there'll be another unmarked grave outside the cabin.*

She had opened the trapdoor soundlessly, allowing light from the candle she held to flicker down about him. He blinked, would have spoken, but Rachel placed an urgent finger to her lips and silenced him. She was wearing a coat and gripping a knife. She lowered herself beside him and without hesitation severed the ropes about his wrists and ankles. He flexed his limbs, gasping with a mixture of pain and relief. He was so stiff she had to help him to his feet and then half drag him out of the cellar. She had snuffed the candle and they stood for a moment in darkness, hardly daring to breathe, then her hand closed over his and he could feel the quivering tension in her. Cautiously she led him across the floor to the door.

Striving to suppress any sound, she eased back the bolts and a moment later they were out beneath the stars. Gratefully, Otis inhaled the cool night air. Now she drew him forward more swiftly. 'There's horses ready in the meadow — and some fresh clothes for you.'

'Why are you doing this?' he gasped. 'Your pa'll go crazy.'

'By the time he finds out, we'll be well away. I can't escape by myself, Johnny No Name. I tried it once, but they caught me. I need your help, maybe worse'n you need mine.'

He did not respond. His brain could hardly grasp what was happening, but he was quite prepared to believe it was a miracle.

The girl had been active. Two horses were ready in the meadow, their saddle-bags bulging with the supplies she had gathered. A man's buckskin coat and a wide-brimmed hat lay on the ground. She picked these up and pushed them into his arms. 'Put them on, quick. We mustn't delay. There's a gun in the saddle-boot and plenty of ammunition.'

Otis nodded and did as he was told. Still stiff, it took him three awkward attempts to mount his horse but at last he succeeded and slipped his feet into the stirrups. The girl had no such difficulty. She had drawn her skirt and coat above her knees and was riding astride. She held up a warning hand for quiet and they listened until they were satisfied that they were undiscovered, then heeled their animals into motion, restraining them to a walk until they were through the meadow gate. Once into open country, their pace quickened to a gallop.

Otis pulled in alongside the girl.

'Where are we going?'

'Into the hills,' she responded. 'We'll be safer there.'

'The hills,' he groaned. 'The Black Hills?' It seemed he was escaping from one nightmare and backtracking into an earlier one — yet as they hastened through the night, he knew she was right. There could be no refuge for them in the town nor any other populated area. Provided they could avoid the Indians, the hills might well offer fewer dangers. He wondered how long it would be before Holy Jack set out to follow their trail, and whether he would dare enter the sacred Indian country. And if Otis and the girl eluded him, and the Sioux, what would they do? Clearly the law would be after Otis — and with a bounty offered for his capture, other men as well. He shook his head in perplexity, then gave up puzzling about the future. All he could do was try to survive, minute by minute, and hope that fate would smile on him. He began to enjoy the feel of a saddled horse beneath him, the great muscles rippling and sliding.

Rachel rode ahead, often glancing over her shoulder to ensure he was coping, the glint of her teeth indicating an encouraging smile. Presently, they reached a crest and reined in to rest their animals. They scrutinized the moon-glazed, silent terrain through which they had passed. Nothing moved and the only sound was the trees talking whisperingly to the breeze. He noticed that Rachel was not riding the Appaloosa. When he asked her about it she said, 'Apple is too recognizable. The Indians would track us down in no time.'

He nodded. She was showing unsuspected astuteness. As they again pushed on, he felt a wave of gratitude towards her. He hoped she would never have cause to regret what she had done for him.

He wondered if she was familiar with these hills — had she ventured into them previously despite the Indian threat? But gradually he concluded that it was the desperate desire to put lengthening mileage between them and the homestead that drove her on.

They took their second stop shortly after dawn, dismounting on the banks of a stream and slackening the girths of their horses, a dapple-grey mare and a big sorrel. As the horses nose-dipped into the clear water, Otis drew the gun out from its scabbard, checked the mechanism and slipped a shell into its breech. It was an old Sharps carbine with an adjustable sight on the stock. He wondered if he would have to kill Holy Jack — with his own gun.

Again he gazed over their back-trail, seeing the vast undulation of hills darkened by pines and cottonwood, all touched by slender fingers of gold slanting through the early mists. Perhaps they would be able to find some hideaway, somewhere to hole up and work out what they could do.

By now, their absence would certainly have been discovered. He sighed at the thought of Holy Jack's fury. But at least he was not breathing down his neck — not for the present.

He glanced across at the girl as she refreshed herself in the stream. She moistened her face, drawing her hands back across her cheeks. Before, he had thought of her as pretty, but now he decided she was beautiful. Her hair was dark, and despite the harassing circumstances of their escape, she had somehow found time to fasten it with a yellow ribbon. She had taken off her coat and as she stooped forward he could see how ripe and attractive her young body was. And yet the innocence in her was frightening. He wondered if she realized the great risk she was taking, entrusting herself to a convicted rapist and killer. He groaned. He looked at his hands. They were stubby and strong. He imagined them ripping at a woman's clothing, gripping her throat . . . Even now he could feel the blood pounding in his head, and it unnerved him. Was it something that he would be unable to control, that would drive him crazy, turning his breathing to a hoarse rasp as lust over-whelmed him?

'Johnny No Name,' she called, unaware of his churning thoughts and somehow amused at the name she had dubbed him, 'there's somethin' I best tell you.'

Her brightly spoken words cleared his brain of the deep waters it was negotiating. 'What's that?'

She reached into the pocket of her dress and extracted a small folded paper. 'It's the map Charlie Casement gave me before he died. I never showed it to Pa. I never showed nobody till now.'

Charlie Casement. To his knowledge, Otis had never known the man, but mention of him brought a sombre reminder of his terrible death, of Holy Jack's maniacal frenzy.

He made no attempt to take the map, so she stepped over to him and held it out. 'It shows where all that money is hidden. Charlie insisted that I keep it, that one day it might be useful.'

Otis took the paper and unfolded it. He saw the rough scrawlings, faint but still discernible — the lines of rivers, of hills and of a high ridge. Halfway along, near a clump of trees, a single arrow pointed to the notation, CASH.

'There's a lot o' money hidden up there,' Rachel murmured. 'Charlie said fifteen thousand dollars. That's what Pa's yearned for these past years. Thank God, he never realized I had this map.'

Otis felt uneasy. The money had been stolen. It would only bring tragedy and death. He had no desire to find it. But Rachel went on, 'Maybe we could reach it, maybe just take a little to help us get away, get to Canada or somewhere Pa can't find us.'

He pondered for a moment, then said, 'Your pa told me three convicts escaped . . . and I was one of them. The other two have most likely reached that money by now.'

'Maybe they have; maybe they haven't. Least we should do is find out.'

She stopped talking. He glanced at her, found himself looking into the disturbing depths of her big blueberry eyes.

'You ain't really that Otis Lockhart, are you?' she asked.

He frowned, his brow creased with emotion. 'Rachel . . . I don't know!'

To his surprise, she slipped her arms around him and hugged him tight, resting her head against his chest. 'You're my Johnny No Name now. I don't care what happened in the past. Anyway, whatever you did, you must have had good reason.'

He was touched by her trust. He smoothed her hair with his hand; it was soft and lustrous — but then deep-down fear stirred him, telling him that no matter how she deluded herself, his true name was Otis Lockhart and he was a murderer of women . . . and why he hadn't dangled on the end of a rope, God only knew! 'Let's press on, Rachel. Your pa's started after us by now.'

She drew back. 'I'm so glad I'm not

alone this time. You'll protect me, won't you, Johnny No Name?'

He bobbed his head, a lump in his throat. He patted her shoulder. 'After what you've done for me, I'll sure do my best.'

She laughed — a happy, girlish laugh.

'Let me clean your head wound,' she said. 'It looks kinda scabby. Then we'll eat. I packed enough food to make sure we don't starve. Not for a while, anyway.'

She washed his head with great care and tenderness. Afterwards, she un-strapped her saddle-bag and extracted bread with meat, corncake and apples. Otis was amazed. She had worked wonders in her preparations. As they chewed, he knew she was watching him. He could feel the warmth of her eyes. When he gazed at her, she grinned. She had a habit of studying him, as if hardly able to believe that he was real. She said, 'First time I've ever met a man like you. Even Charlie . . . well, he was different. And I want you to know, I don't really hanker after that money . . . but it's our only chance.'

Otis took a deep breath. Our only chance. He nodded reluctantly.

Within minutes, they were on the move once more, the hills rising about them. He couldn't somehow stop thinking about his companion. She was little more than half his age. She reminded him of a fawn, zestful and glad to be alive. I must never hurt her, he thought, never!

The heat of the sun rose and sometimes they had to shade their eyes from its brightness. Throughout the morning, they pressed onward, following the line of a stream, frequently riding in the water to obscure their trail. They passed through meadows, pink, purple and white with flowers, sweetening the air with their redolence. Sometimes she examined the map but soon she said it was firmly fixed in her mind. Often, they reined in to gaze back, but they saw no sign of human life, though nature was vibrant with the song of magpies, thrushes and redwings, and the trees were alive with chipmunks and squirrels. Later, when they gazed across at an adjacent hill, they saw darkness blanketing the slope. At first Otis thought it was cloud shadow, but then, glancing up, he saw how the sky was pure azure, the sun a naked bronze totally unshielded by cloud. He swung his gaze back to the far slope.

'Buffalo,' Rachel murmured, 'a huge herd of buffalo.'

Otis nodded. 'No wonder the Indians love to hunt here.'

As their horses plodded on, she told him about her mother and what a gentle woman she'd been, never retaliating to the awful treatment dished out by Holy Jack. She told him how frequently the root-cellar had been used as a place of confinement. On occasions both she and her mother had been secured in there to contemplate their sins. But after the death of his wife, the old man had favoured a thick leather strap with which to chastise.

'You're so different from him,' Otis commented. 'Is he your real pa, Rachel?'

She gave him a surprised look. 'Well, he's always been around, so I guess that makes him my real pa. What else can make a man your real pa?'

He felt bewildered by her naivete. 'Haven't you ever seen your animals mating?'

'Mating?' she queried. 'You mean sins of the flesh?

'Sort of.'

'Pa would never let me near when they did that, nor when they birthed. He said he didn't want to put no ideas in my head; them things weren't for young girls to see.'

Otis said, 'I guess he's your real pa right enough,' and left it at that.

'Johnny No Name,' she said with intensity.

'Yup.'

'You got the most beautiful lips.'

By noon on that first day of freedom, they had made good progress. It was clear that Rachel was well-used to horseback, for she handled her bay with confidence. As his aches eased, Otis found the girl's ebullient manner lifting his spirits, and he was again amazed at how a young person so narrow in experience, living in fear of a vile father, could radiate such joy. Clearly the prospect of escape had been like a revitalizing stimulant for her.

He also pondered on himself. Perhaps the blow to his head had somehow destroyed the evil that had previously plagued his soul. But how could he be sure? Would there come a moment when his sanity snapped, when he reverted to the devil incarnate? He shuddered and recalled how a question had probed into his mind more than once. What was her sweet body like beneath the coarse cotton of her dress? How wondrous it would be to press his lips to her breasts! He tore his eyes away from the easy sway of her back and trim waist as she rode ahead and in so doing, his glance took in the timbered slopes of the pass they had recently come up. Thoughts of the girl were immediately banished from his mind.

He had been startled by a sudden stab of brilliance that was gone immediately. Instinct warned him that had he looked a fraction of a second before, he would have spotted something more revealing. His mouth had gone dry. He strained his eyes, peering at the mottled, secretive mixture of pine fronds, undergrowth and shadow some mile away, seeking some sign of movement but seeing none. He was conscious that both he and the girl would be clearly visible from down the pass.

'What is it?' she called, reining in her bay.

'Something glinted from down there, Rachel. Could've been the sun reflecting on an eye-glass.'

'Pa's got an eye-glass,' she said, her happiness displaced by sudden fear.

Together, they studied the distant slope, but nothing showed and he wondered if his senses had been playing tricks. He cursed himself for alarming the girl.

They moved on, following a game trail through airily-spaced conifers. Occasional unexpected breaks of grassland gave forth to cliff drops and startling vistas. Eventually they descended into a valley. They glanced back frequently. He doubted that the Indians would have an eye-glass; but, according to Rachel, Holy Jack had one, also no doubt any bounty hunters who might have taken up the trail.

During the late afternoon, they reached a wide plateau which they crossed and came to a small gorge. They were thankful that the mosquitoes were less troublesome now that they were in higher country. Otis decided to make camp for the night. They were both tense and weary. They unsaddled and hobbled the horses where the verdure was good, then they ate their own cold supper. After this, Otis undertook a brief survey of the local terrain.

He saw rabbit droppings and thought about making a snare. It occurred to him that he could use the whangs from his buckskin coat, tie them together and make a slipknot loop at the end. But he was saved the chore. Rachel, ever resourceful, had some string in her saddle-bag.

He got to work, fashioning a loop and allowing himself about six feet pulling length. He placed the loop around the edge of a much-used burrow and waited, with the string fastened to his thumb. He was incredibly lucky. Within ten minutes a large, unsuspecting rabbit popped its head out for an exploratory look. Otis yanked on the snare and felt it go taut. He pulled like a fisherman dragging in his catch. He had caught himself some squealing, fresh meat for the morrow.

They had stopped near a cliff top and he decided that this would be a good spot from which to keep watch.

For an hour they sat close, their backs against the heaped tack. With the air cooling, she hugged herself to him, grateful for the warmth of his body. He told her that he must keep watch and would do so from the cliff's top. She nodded. 'I'll take over after a few hours. You need sleep just as much as me. And Johnny No Name . . . I've never been so happy in my life. I feel so safe with you.'

He felt unworthy of her. If she had known the thoughts that eddied in his head, her trust might have turned to hate. He sat a while longer and presently realized that she was asleep. He gently rested her down, covered her with a blanket, making sure she was comfortable. He felt almost like a father, tucking his child into bed. Then, gathering up the carbine, he climbed to the cliff top and hunkered down.

For a moment it seemed he heard murmuring voices entwined with the breeze but he convinced himself that this time it was his senses playing tricks. Above him the moon cruised like a great luminous eye, flooding the earth with its silvery and eerie glow. In daytime, this country could seem like bliss, with its sweet streams, colourful flowers and green, pine-cloaked hills, but come darkness everything changed. The Indians claimed that the hills were inhabited by the spirits of the dead. He shivered. Maybe they were right.

Midnight came and went uneventfully. For hours his senses remained sharp, but eventually his thoughts intruded. It seemed incredible that his skills, his instincts, his worldliness, remained undamaged, while his knowledge of himself, of his life before he had clawed himself from that grave, had been sluiced away. He wondered how much more tortured he would be had it not been. He tried to recall the faces of the two convicts who, according to Holy Jack, had escaped with him — but not an inkling of their appearance came to him.

He could feel exhaustion in his bones and fought to keep awake. When the voice sounded, he came alert guiltily. 'Johnny No Name, guess you better bed down for an hour or so, else you'll fall asleep in the saddle tomorrow.'

'You need rest more 'n me,' he argued, but Rachel laughed and took the gun from him. 'I'll keep watch,' she said. 'I'll wake you at dawn.'

He hesitated, then decided that she was right — as usual.

'Good night, Johnny No Name,' she whispered, and her hand touched his face, her fingers exploring his beard. Impulsively, she drew his lips to hers and she pressed her pliant body against him. For all her inexperience, she knew how to kiss. He had the feeling that she'd have eaten him had not laughter got the better of them.

'Who taught you to kiss like that?' he gasped breathlessly.

She touched her tingling lips. 'It was wonderful. It just comes . . . natural.'

He turned away, his senses still pounding, but she grasped his arm and drew him back.

'It's the other things I need to know about,' she whispered. 'The things Pa calls 'sins of the flesh'.'

'They'll come natural too, Rachel.'

'Maybe, maybe not. Maybe, if I wait, I'll be too old to enjoy them. I need somebody to show me, Johnny No Name. Will you do it?'

'One day,' he said, 'one day I'll tell you all you need to know.'

'*Show* not tell,' she persisted.

He was breathing heavily. He wanted her all right; he wanted her now. But all he did was nod and murmur, 'If that's what you really wish. One day, maybe,' and he gave her hand a squeeze and left her, knowing that she would be angry with him. As he descended to the gorge, he comforted himself with the thought that perhaps he had been right. Perhaps the blow he had received on the head, had not only destroyed his memory, but had jarred the wickedness from his soul as well.

He checked the horses. They were standing silently in the darkness, hock-deep in lush meadow grass. He rubbed their noses, murmuring to them softly. Satisfied that all was well, he returned to the meagre camp. He pulled the blanket over him and closed his eyes. His senses were still pounding from Rachel's nearness. He imagined he could still smell the fresh womanly tang of her in his nostrils. One day, maybe, he thought and drifted into sleep.

A half-hour later the girl's scream cut through the darkness, jolting him to horrified wakefulness.

6

Grinner Willoughby was sleeping fitfully and he grunted from time to time. In his dream, he was forcing earth into Otis's mouth and nostrils, packing it tight in an effort to stop him breathing, then, when he could swear that Otis's chest was no longer rising and falling, he filled in the grave. He even made a slight mound on its top, stamping it firm with his feet. But as he gazed at it, he saw it moving up and down. My God, Otis was still breathing!

Willoughby awoke with a snort, sweating and trembling. For a time he struggled with his senses, then gradually he saw the dream for what it was — sheer fantasy. He was glad that, in reality, he had not filled in the grave despite Will Selby's wishes. At least Otis's dying would have been gentle, his wheezing fading gently away as the life slipped from him — that was if the Indians hadn't molested him.

'Never knew a man like you for makin' so much damned noise when he's sleepin',' Will Selby complained. He was sitting a few yards away, his ape-like face showing up gaunt in the moonlight. The pistol lay ready in his lap. They had stopped at a point where boulders lay circled in a dip along the crest of a hill. Selby hardly slept at all himself, but kept alert, anxious to make sure no untoward events prevented him from reaching his goal — the cave where the cash was hidden.

'Funny how those red varmints have disappeared since you shot that fella in the warbonnet.' Willoughby rubbed his face with his hand. It wasn't any fun to have his mouth stretched in a permanent grin. It made his entire jaw ache.

Selby spat. 'It ain't normal for Injuns to give up so easy. When you don't hear 'em, that's most likely when they're around. We got to keep our eyes peeled, Grinner. That's why we got to stick to the ridges where we can get a good view. I . . . ' His voice died out.

'What is it?' Willoughby hissed.

Selby didn't answer. He was holding his breath, tilting his head on one side to better his hearing. After a moment he whispered, 'Figured I heard a horse whinny. Somewhere down below us.'

Both men strained their ears into the night, their eyes probing the terrain. The moon was cold and full above them. Presently they heard the triple-bark of a coyote from somewhere off to the north.

'Maybe you imagined it,' Willoughby murmured.

Selby shook his head. He checked his pistol. 'I don't know. I guess we'll push on before dawn. Nothin' must stop us from reachin' that cave.'

'You got a damned fine memory to remember how we get there, Will, with no map or nothin'.'

Selby allowed himself a thin smile. 'I'll find it OK.' He knew he would recognize the place where those twin peaks reared and the trees were lined like a phalanx of charging cavalry. He had dreamed about it so often. He would run his hands through those sweet bundles of bills, feel the ecstasy that would make those prison-years worthwhile. He reckoned three more days should see them at the cave. He and Willoughby would be able to carry the bulk of the money; the rest they would leave for the proverbial rainy day. Had Otis still been with them, he would have carried his share and they might have managed the lot. Once they had reached some place of safety, Selby would have disposed of Otis in the same way he had the prison-guard kid. It was incredible how the quick snap of a pistol could solve so many problems. Of course, Willoughby would have taken it badly. For some reason he had taken a liking to the red-bearded rapist, but he would have seen sense after a while. He always did.

Willoughby had removed his socks and boots, was gingerly feeling his broken skin. All this walking had given him terrible blisters. Now they were seeping pus. 'Damned feet,' he grumbled. 'They feel they're on fire. I'll be glad to get a horse under me again.' He replaced his ragged socks, then asked, 'After we got the cash, what'll we do?'

Selby had given it a great deal of thought. 'Figure we'll go to Oregon, take a boat from Portland or some such place. We'll have to think up some new fancy names to call ourselves. We'll go to South America, maybe Brazil. They won't find us down there.'

'With that cash,' Willoughby said, 'we can become respectable gentlemen. We won't need to do no more crime.'

Selby smiled again. 'Not less'n we feel like it. Maybe if there's a bank crying out to be robbed, we could take up part-time employment.'

Willoughby pondered, then said, 'We'll have to make doggone sure we don't rob the bank where we've lodged our finances. That'd be the last straw — robbin' ourselves!' He laughed at his joke.

Selby wasn't amused. 'First thing I'm gonna do is get myself a woman or two. We been denied for far too long. It ain't good for a man.'

He growled with pleasure at the prospect of female company. 'Yes, you and me been too long without, Grinner. Now you get back to your sweet dreams. I'll just take a mosey around.' Uneasily he added, 'I swear blind that was a horse I heard.'

He drew his pistol and eased off into the shadows.

He circled their position for a half-hour, moving silently through the darkness of the trees, pausing frequently to listen. He began to doubt that it was a horse's whinny he had heard. Maybe it had been some wild creature, though he didn't know what. He was anxious to press on for the cave, but Willoughby was slowing their progress down, constantly complaining about his blisters and wanting to stop. Prison life must have made him soft. Maybe they'd hole up at the cave for a few days and give him time to recover. It would also give Selby time to set traps for fresh meat.

Confident that immediate danger did not threaten, Selby decided it was time to rouse Willoughby, to push on. Already the moon was long-gone and the heavens were showing pale along the eastern skyline. He returned to the ring of boulders where Willoughby lay. For once he wasn't snorting and grunting in his sleep. He was sprawled face down, unmoving, and Selby was cursing him for being so easily crept up upon. Somebody could have slipped a knife between his ribs before he realized.

Then he noticed how something was protruding from Willoughby's back and, when he touched it, he felt its sharpness and his hand came away moist — the shock cut through him and he knew that the moisture was blood. He rolled the body over and saw the feathered stub protruding from the chest. An arrow had skewered right through him.

Selby's gaze swung to Willoughby's

face. The grin had gone; the flesh was hanging like an empty bladder over his cheeks and jaw because it was no longer pulled upward by natural tautness. Willoughby's scalp had been sliced away, leaving the pale top of his skull exposed.

Selby unleashed an obscenity and crouched over the corpse, gazing furtively around, the pistol raised, the words he'd uttered earlier that night stabbing at his mind: When you don't hear 'em, that's most likely when they're around. He sensed that another arrow might come flying through the gloom at any moment — and this time it would have his name on it.

★   ★   ★

Holy Jack! The name stabbed at Otis with the sharpness of an Indian lance. He was on his feet instantly, stumbling clear of the blanket, his heart hammering in his chest. The girl's scream seemed to reverberate in the pre-dawn gloom. Behind, in the meadow, the horses had set up an alarmed whinnying and were plunging against their hobbles. Otis mounted the slope in great leaps, tearing through the brush, wishing that he still had the gun. Reaching the top, his frantic eyes seized on to the shadowy figure ahead of him. A man was crouched down, pinioning a struggling figure to the ground — Rachel! Her attacker had encircled her with rope, was drawing it tight when Otis dove at him. He grabbed the man's shoulders, dragged him back, realizing that it was not Holy Jack he was fighting. He also knew that the stranger had snatched a knife from its sheath, would twist round to make a thrust.

Otis got his forearm across his adversary's throat, preventing him from turning, trying to choke him into submission, immediately sensing that this would be impossible. For a second they were locked in semi-stalemate, then, with incredible strength, the stranger forced himself up, lifting Otis with him. Otis felt the agonizing stab of a spur in his groin, driven with the impact of a horse's kick. The shock loosened his hold. The other man was free of him immediately, twisting around, the two facing each other in that misty, early light like feuding stags.

As they drew apart, the stranger laughed, arrogance spreading across his dark face. With the knife, he slashed little crosses in the air, teasing Otis. He was taller than he looked because of the great breadth and bulk of him. A goatee decorated his chin in the fashion of a Conquistador. His jacket and leather chivarras were embellished with heavy, side buckles. He was clearly Mexican, his thick accent leaving no doubt. 'A fight to the death, eh *amigo!*' he cried out, and there was an exultancy in him, a relish for the kill.

He sprang, the knife held high. Otis flung up his hands, half warding off the blade. Even so he felt a sharp sting across his shoulder, knew his shirt had been slashed — and his arm beneath.

He snarled in anguish, grappled to seize the Mexican's throat, failing because his grip was too slippery. He rammed his knee upwards but did not connect. The Mexican was twisting and leaping, surprisingly nimble for his size; it was almost as if he was dancing the fandango, the flash of his teeth ushering his mocking laugh. Otis yelled, 'You're crazy!' and made a wild lunge. His fist, swung with utter venom, cleaved thin air and he stumbled off-balance as the other man pranced to the side and spat out the words: 'Eet is too easy, *amigo!*'

Again they faced each other, their breath rasping in unison, the Mexican's still edged with his mocking laugh. He was like a cat, toying with his victim before the kill. It was clear he favoured the knife, but Otis noticed there was a pistol holstered at his hip.

The Mexican crouched low, weaving back and forth, then he charged again. This time, Otis got hold of his knife arm, forcing it up, coming jowl to jowl with his attacker, feeling the burn of his murderous intent. But it was the Mexican's teeth which broke the grip; he sank them into Otis's neck. Otis twisted away, releasing his grip on the man's arm, realizing that he had surrendered the initiative. The Mexican swung his left fist, catching Otis across the head.

Otis went down, dropping to all fours. He sprang to the side to avoid another knife thrust, then, crouching ready for the next onslaught, he realized that his hand had clawed over a rock the size of an apple. There was no time to hurl it. Instead he drove it into the Mexican's face, feeling it connect solidly, hearing the splinter of teeth and jawbone, knowing that the smile would be gone.

Amazingly, the man stayed on his feet, though the knife had slipped from his grasp. His eyes glinted hatred from his smashed face. His hand was sliding the pistol from its leather holster at his hip. Now, he was no longer playing games. But Otis saw the dazed sway in him, knew that only a scant second remained before the gun was levelled and blasted off. He straightened his legs in a desperate jump, launching himself head-first into his enemy's midriff, just above the metal buckle of the gun-belt. The crunching impact stunned him, cracking his neck. He fell, reeling from his own impetus, but somehow aware that the Mexican had tumbled backwards.

It seemed an age before his addled senses resumed any coherence. He was conscious of pain in his head and neck. He moved his head, grunting with the suffering it caused. He supported the back of his neck with his hand. He flexed his jaw and moved his head again and the pain was receding. Thank God he hadn't broken his neck. He glanced around, aware that dawn was sifting in. Where's that bastard Mexican? He was nowhere to be seen.

Then another question loomed in his mind: What had happened to Rachel? The fight had carried him well away from where he had last seen her. He forced himself up, suddenly oblivious to his pain, or the fact that the Mexican might come bounding back.

He found her groaning and helpless, lying gagged and secured with rope. He ripped the gag away, then tore at the knots with his fingers, cursing at their tightness but at last slackening them.

'Where is he?' she was gasping. 'Are you all right?'

He nodded. 'Rachel, I don't know where he is. He vanished after I hit him with a rock.'

She glanced around, her eyes big with fear. 'I'm sorry. I must've been dozing. He crept up on me, grabbed me before I could do anything.'

'You screamed. If you hadn't, we'd be finished now.'

'Thank God you heard me.' Then she asked, 'Who was he?'

'Bounty hunter for sure,' he replied. 'He must've trailed us for quite a while. Where's the gun?'

She pointed to where the weapon lay

and he retrieved it, checked the mechanism. 'Let's find him,' he grunted. 'Keep close to me.'

She scrambled up and together they crept forward, and a moment later Otis guessed what had happened. The fight had taken them far closer to the cliff edge than he had realized. The Mexican, reeling from the head-butt, must have stepped backwards . . . and plunged into the abyss. Otis and Rachel peered downward; the drop was considerable. At the base of the cliff, ground mist lay in swirls, but through this hundreds of white objects jutted up.

At first Otis was puzzled, then, in a hushed voice, Rachel murmured, 'Buffalo bones. The Indians must've used this cliff to stampede the herds over.'

Otis whistled through his teeth. 'A buffalo cemetery. I hope that his bones will rot with theirs. But we can't be sure.'

For a good five minutes they clung to each other in awe. Nothing moved below them. Rachel whispered, 'Should we go down, see if we can find him?'

Otis had had enough of this crazy chilli-eater. He never wanted to see hide nor hair of him again, but the girl persisted. 'If we don't actually see his body, we won't know whether he's still comin' after us. We could never rest. We've got to make sure he's dead.'

Otis hesitated. Again he was impressed by her practicality. He felt pretty certain that nobody could survive the fall from the cliff . . . so perhaps there was nothing to fear. At least it would put Rachel's mind at rest.

They moved along the rim for maybe a hundred yards, until the drop shallowed out into a steep but descendable slope. Otis led the way, holding the girl's arm with one hand, cradling the carbine in the other. They clambered through a series of rocky outcrops until they reached the valley floor. It was a sinister place, made unworldly by the carpet of mist. Soon, they were stepping amid the thick scattering of buffalo bones and horns. Otis shuddered. It must have been a fearsome sight to see hundreds of animals, mad with fright, being stampeded over the cliff top like an avalanche, plummeting downward, crashing to death or terrible injury. The noise of thundering hooves and brassy bellows must have been deafening. Afterwards, it would have been easy for the Indians to move amongst the beasts, butchering them with knives and lances, devouring raw brains and intestines, taking what they needed of meat, skins, hooves and bone, but still leaving plenty for the wolves and buzzards to pick clean.

Rachel stayed close as they searched the dismal graveyard. There was a throat-gagging, stale smell still lingering about the place, though it must have been many years since the wholesale killing had occurred. They discovered no sign of the Mexican. With the new day taking a firmer hold, they glanced upward at the towering cliff. Across its face there were bushes and a few ledges jutting out. Otis wondered uneasily if these might have offered some hand-hold, something that might have arrested the Mexican's fall. He pondered for a moment, then dismissed the idea.

'We best go on, Rachel,' he said. 'We can't waste any more time here. We . . .'

'*Johnny!*'

He glimpsed her fear-crazed face and instinctively lunged to the side, conscious that the murderous swing of something heavy had cleaved the air inches from his head. Momentum had caused the Mexican, looking like a monster risen from the dead, to blunder past. He was screaming and swinging a huge buffalo leg-bone, like a scythe. He twisted, his eyes seething hatred, his breath pumping out in misty blasts, then suddenly he charged at Otis again, the bone held high.

Otis brought the carbine up, one-handed, his finger snatching at the trigger. The gun blasted off, its lead ripping into the Mexican's chest, halting his attack, hurling him back and down. The bone curled from his grasp in a graceful loop.

Rachel was shrieking in horror, her hands pressed against her cheeks. Otis stood with the sweat streaming over him, his ears ringing with the detonation; his jangling senses gradually steadied, but his legs were trembling as he went forward and stooped over the bounty hunter.

When he straightened up, he turned to the girl. 'You wanted him dead, Rachel. Now you can be sure.'

She had quieted. All she could do was nod and reach out to be comforted by the man she called Johnny No Name. Presently she murmured, 'You've been hurt. You must let me take care of you.'

7

'Whoever piled them rocks on him made a lame fist of it,' Holy Jack said.

Jacob gazed at the bloody stump of a foot which stuck out where the heap of rocks had been disturbed. He felt sick. 'Wolves've gnawed half his foot off! P-probably would've dug the rest of the bo-body up, if we hadn't c-come along.'

'Weren't wolves what did the chewin'!' the old man retorted impatiently. 'They might've scraped at the rocks, but wolves won't touch raw human meat. Too salty. It was heathen buzzards what pecked the toes off.'

Father and son stood gazing down at the untidy heap of rocks their tracking had led them to. Standing side by side in their slouch hats and dark-greasy buckskins, they resembled a couple of crows. The focus of their attention had clearly been intended as some sort of grave, made to keep off wild creatures, but, having been poorly fashioned, it had failed dismally. Holy Jack dropped to his haunches, began shifting the remaining rocks.

'What you g-gonna do, Pa?' Jacob asked uneasily.

'Dig him out. See who he is, though I've got a sneakin' idea.'

'I ain't n-never been fond of digging c-corpses out of graves.'

Holy Jack snorted testily. 'That's 'cos you ain't never done it, son. Anyway, you're too soft, same as your depraved sister. Less'n we can get her back, she'll rot in purgatory for certain.' He continued to move the rocks away, gradually uncovering the corpse. Jacob could smell it and it made gruesome viewing, so he turned away.

They had left the smallholding soon after pacifying the Indians and persuading them to depart. Iron Shield and his braves had left for their village on the Powder River. Once they arrived there, with news of Red Bonnet's death and the intrusion of *wasicuns* into the sacred country, it was likely that a storm of Indian reprisal would be unleashed.

Holy Jack had found the trail of his daughter and Otis Lockhart easily enough and had followed it into the hills, cursing Rachel every step of the way. He was also fuming about the theft of the supplies, horses and carbine. How could a fine-reared girl like Rachel, who'd been shielded from the wickedness of the world, turn so bad?

The old man was an expert at reading sign, boasting he could follow a woodtick on solid rock. He was adept at spotting crushed grass, snapped twigs, hoof and foot-prints and horse droppings which told him how long it was since the animals had passed.

But despite his skills, he had somehow got thrown off-track and for a day and a half they had searched around. Eventually, they discovered where somebody had camped — but it hadn't been Rachel and Lockhart. It had been two men travelling on foot.

Holy Jack had cackled with delight. These must be the other convicts, Selby and Willoughby. He figured if he trailed them, they'd lead him to the hidden cache of money. No doubt Rachel and Lockhart were heading the same way — but if necessary, he could deal with them later. He'd always felt certain that Lockhart knew the location of the cash perfectly well despite his playing dumb.

It had been a surprise when, in the afternoon of the next day, they stumbled across the grave, close to the ring of boulders.

Holy Jack showed no disgust as he pulled away the rocks. In fact he grunted with satisfaction as he saw what he had suspected. The body was clad in a soiled arrowhead suit. He dragged it out from under the remaining rocks, noting how an arrow-feather protruded from the chest. Must have been Running Elk who killed him, he thought, remembering how Iron Shield had told him how the young warrior had gone after the convicts, bent on revenge. With the back of his hand, he dusted off the earth from the discoloured mess of the face and studied it closely. It was as ugly as sin, the flesh gone all slack because of the scalping; even so, Holy Jack was confident it remained recognizable and would provide adequate proof as to the identity of the corpse. He went down the slope to where his and Jacob's horses were grazing. From his saddle-bag he extracted a butchering knife, thanking the Lord that he had had the fore-sight to bring it, then he went back to the body.

'What you g-gonna do, Pa?' Jacob enquired; his mouth lolled open in expectation of something ghastly. The old man paused impatiently and glared at his son. 'You got the intelligence of a three-day-old hog, Jacob. We got to have some evidence. There ain't no better way of provin' who he is *and* that he's dead, than by presentin' his head to the law. They'll have no option but to pay out the bounty. Remember them posters said 'dead or alive'. If, by any chance, we don't find the cache of money, then at least we'll have somethin'. Anyway, I can't waste no more time explainin' things to you. Fetch me that sack you got in your saddle-bag.' He commenced his grisly task.

Of late, Jacob had become disgusted by his father's behaviour. He kept a list of grudges in his mind, starting with when the old man had driven their ma to her grave. Then had come the murder of Charlie Casement whom Jacob, as well as Rachel, had taken a liking to. Next there'd been the killing of Elijah, the old dog . . . and of course Jacob knew that his father was the root-cause of Rachel's unhappiness. Now it seemed the old man had stooped even lower in desecrating the body of a departed soul. But Jacob had never revealed his deepest thoughts; it would have been more than his life was worth.

When his son returned with the sack, Holy Jack was busy hacking through the dead man's neck. It was downright tough, especially when he reached the bone, but he persevered with the task.

Jacob watched aghast. 'Oh G-God, Pa. How can you d-do such a thing!' He felt so sickened he hardly heard his father's angry admonition, 'Jacob . . . what right do you have to take the Lord's name in vain! I may curse, but I don't never blaspheme. I truly don't know what my family is comin' to.'

* * *

After they had left the Mexican's body to rot and be scavenged among the buffalo bones, they discovered his fiesty dun horse with a fancy Mother Hubbard saddle, tethered in the brush. Its saddle-bag yielded a good supply of Indian-style pemmican — pounded meat mixed with fat and berries. The bounty hunter had done them a good turn, supplying them with food and an extra mount.

When they paused to fill their canteen from a stream, Rachel examined his head, cuts and bruises. With deft fingers, she made sure they were clean and refastened the head bandage as best she could. 'You'll not die, Johnny No Name,' she declared. 'Leastways not from these hurts.'

She kissed his lips like a naughty schoolgirl, and turned away laughing.

As they pressed on, Otis noted how the country was changing. The ponderosas had given way to tall spruce, alive with scampering chipmunks, and there were fewer open meadows apart from in the base of the valley, along the floor of which the river cleaved its way like a silky ribbon. Ahead, the grey crags showed closer, today shrouded by low cloud, and it was there that the cave awaited.

That afternoon, Otis built a snakehole fire, ensuring that its output of smoke was minimal. They roasted the rabbit and enjoyed their meal, sucking the bones. Then they resumed their journey.

Several times, Rachel reached into

her skirt pocket, consulted her map and pointed the way forward. Meanwhile a sense of distaste was growing in Otis — a conviction that no good would come of the ill-gotten loot which had already cost several men their lives. Yet he saw the wisdom of the girl's argument — that with money their chances of escape would be greatly enhanced. In consequence he tried to ignore his misgivings and allowed Rachel to plot their route while he kept an alert eye on the surrounding terrain, the carbine slanted across his knees as he rode. He had no wish to be surprised again by bounty hunters, Indians, Holy Jack or anybody else. Presently they encountered a grove of wild plum trees. They picked the ripe fruit and rode on, enjoying its sweetness.

Otis glanced at the girl, seeing how amusement bubbled in her eyes; her cheeks were shiny with plum juice, the exuberant, vital spark of her youth not dimmed by her drab, travel-soiled dress. She gave him an impish grin, then grew serious. 'When we get away, clear away I mean, maybe in Canada . . . will you stay with me? I got nobody else.'

He hesitated. There might be other women in his life, he had no way of telling, but he concluded that it no longer mattered. If he escaped, disappearing into some far off place, his past would be gone — if not in the minds of others, certainly in his own mind.

He said, 'I'm old enough to be your father, Rachel.'

'I wish you were my father; then we would be a family, and never, never leave each other. I need you.' She bit her nether lip, then said, 'And I love you, Johnny No Name!'

'Do you know what love is?' he asked.

'Yes I do. I can feel it inside me. But I want you to teach me more.'

He glowed with a sudden warmth for her. Seeing a bright red flower growing from the grass, he slid side-ways in his saddle, reached down and plucked it. He presented it to her. 'I'll stay with you, Rachel,' he promised. 'I need you just as much as you need me.'

As he drew his hand away, she said, 'But how about love? Do you love me . . . just a little bit?'

'More than a little bit, much more.'

'Then show me,' she retorted, 'show me tonight!'

He was about to respond when the crack of a shot cut sharply through the day's tranquillity and they reined in their horses, alarmed. 'Came from ahead of us,' Otis said in a hushed voice. 'Maybe half a mile. Seemed like a handgun.'

A minute later the shot was repeated.

★ ★ ★

Earlier that afternoon, Will Selby had been feeling the strain. On foot, he'd covered many miles and he was confident that by tomorrow evening he would reach the cave. But the tension of having to watch his back constantly for fear that the Indian was lurking around, stringing an arrow to his bow, kept his spine twitching and his nerves on edge. Even the swoosh of a bird would have him throwing himself down, his gun ready. But what sickened him the most was the loss of Grinner Willoughby. He'd never grieved for any other human being, except his mother. Willoughby, for all his irritating faults, was the best friend he'd ever had. He'd grown used to that hideous grin. They'd been together during the war years and on a hundred escapades since, keeping a hair's breadth ahead of the law. They'd shared their women, their loot, their liquor, good times and bad, even their eventual imprisonment — everything. Selby had gunned down many men, and would have killed more had it not been for Willoughby's restraining and often cautious influence. They'd worked well together. Now it had taken a damned red-belly to destroy their partnership.

Selby had done his best for Willough-by's body, piling rocks over it to discourage scavengers — but it was a harrowing task, knowing that the killer

136

was somewhere out there in the night, hankering, no doubt, to complete the job he'd started. He'd finished as quickly as possible, then left that place, dodging through the forest, constantly glancing over his shoulder, sensing that the Indian would follow him and strike whenever it suited him.

The following night he'd hidden himself in a thicket, but he couldn't sleep. He ran his hand through the tangled mass of his hair, reminding himself how attached he was to his scalp. He swore no filthy savage was going to peel it off. As he tried to rest, the past kept drifting into his mind, coming as clear as if it was happening all over again.

He was once more at the cave and they had just concealed the cash. There had been six of them, all members of his gang. And when the loot was cached away, Selby had glanced at his companions and figured what a fool he was being. Any of them might return here before he did and help themselves to the fortune that he and Willoughby had planned so carefully to acquire.

By the next day, as they travelled north from the cave, Selby had made his decision. When they stopped for the night, Willoughby moved off to stand guard on a nearby hillock. The rest tried to get some sleep around their small fire — all except Selby. He drew his two handguns on the pretext of cleaning them. Instead, he carefully checked the chambers, then he thumbed back the hammers, raised the guns and pressed the triggers. He unleashed a maelstrom of lead into his unsuspecting companions as they lay in their blankets, his shots coming so fast they didn't have time to react — apart from one man.

Charlie Casement somehow survived, leaping up and racing like a pronghorn into the trees. Selby stormed after him, ramming more shells into his pistols and blasting away, but to no avail. Casement, always slick, got clear and Selby never saw him again. Later, he consoled himself with the hope that the Indians might have caught him. That being hopefully so, it left only him and Willoughby to share the cash between them.

Of course, Willoughby grumbled about the killings. He always barked at the knot, but he eventually saw the sense of it. As usual.

That had been four years ago.

Now, with dawn sifting its pale light through the overhead fronds, Selby roused himself sluggishly from his thicket, but soon his mood brightened. Tonight, he thought, tonight, I'll reach the cave. He grinned at the prospect. Once he had money in his pocket, he'd be able to take his pick of women — women who wouldn't be turned off by his ape-like face, women with warm breasts and churning, welcoming thighs who would respond eagerly to the hunger in him.

Even so, he wished Willoughby was still around to help carry those banknotes. Willoughby with his sore feet and idiot grin — and maybe a couple of horses as well.

★ ★ ★

Running Elk told himself that this would be the day when he took his second *wasicun* scalp. He held his dark head high, taking profound pride in his feral manhood. He had enjoyed stalking this man, at first wondering where he was going with such relentless determination — but now the young warrior's patience had waned and he longed to complete his quest and return to the village with two scalps at his belt, to be acclaimed for his courage and fortitude. Only then would the killing of Red Bonnet be truly avenged; only then would the chief's spirit be wafted away, to travel up the great Hanging Road and live peacefully in the land of the Wise One Above.

In consequence, Running Elk prepared himself for conflict. He took out the small bag in which he carried his warpaint, mixed the vivid colours with animal fat and applied them to his face and body, using a pool to reflect his image. Once satisfied, he turned to his pony, circling its eyes with white clay, daubing its flanks with the blood-red imprint of his hand and tying feathers into its mane and tail. Thus bedecked, warrior and pony went forth to kill the *wasicun* intruder.

The keen eyes of the Indian had no trouble in finding the trail. White people moved about the land with the subtlety of a rutting bull. In the afternoon, as he reached the crest of a hill upslope of a stream, he spotted his quarry. He immediately backtracked, tethered his pony and, hugging the ground, returned to his vantage point. Selby was hunkered down, taking a breather in a grassy nook, his back pressed against a large boulder. He kept glancing furtively from side to side. Running Elk noticed the fine pistol he possessed and grunted with delight as he anticipated owning it soon. He selected an arrow from his quiver, touching it with his lips before fitting it to his bow. He paused, whispering a quick prayer to the Spirits, then he rose to his knees. He squinted along the feathered shaft, drew back the bowstring to its full extent and let go.

The hum of the arrow had Selby dodging to the side, but he was too late to avoid the impact. With an agonized cry, he stood up, staggered and fell, concealed by the boulder — apart from his boots which jutted out.

The Indian scrambled down the intervening slope, casting aside the bow and drawing his knife, his youthful impetuousness blinding him to all considerations other than the lifting of his second scalp. Accordingly, it came as a shock when he rounded the boulder to find himself blinking into the ugly black borehole of the pistol he'd earlier coveted. Selby was sitting up, the arrow jutting from his thigh, his finger tightening on the trigger. The gun went off at point-blank range, blasting the Indian back, blood spurting from his chest. He hit the ground, lay writhing for a moment, then his head came up to meet Selby's merciless stare.

Gritting his teeth against his agony, he launched into his death song, intoning it with all his remaining strength.

As much to shut off the singing as anything else, Selby hobbled painfully across to the Indian, touched the pistol to his head and blew out his brains, thankful, as the ring of the detonation subsided, that the dirge was silenced. He noticed something fastened to the Indian's belt. He cursed, then reached forward to touch it. It was Willoughby's scalp.

He lowered himself to the ground. He grimaced at the sight of the arrow jutting from his thigh. Blood had turned his trouser leg into a sodden mess.

★　★　★

Otis and Rachel listened for more shots but none came. 'We'd best push on,' Rachel said. 'It could be Injuns, and we don't want nothin' to do with them.'

'That shot came from a handgun,'

Otis murmured. 'Indians don't normally favour handguns. Could be we're catching up with my convict friends. Perhaps they took a pot shot at a rabbit.'

The girl shook her head, not happy. 'Maybe it's Pa — and I sure don't want to meet with him.'

But Otis was thinking that if it was Selby and Willoughby, seeing them again could spark his memory. Knowledge of his past might not bring him much joy but at least he would know where he stood. Anyway, the two men with whom he'd escaped must be his associates, if not his friends. They were in a similar predicament to his own, with a bounty on their heads for recapture, and survival might come easier if they stuck together.

'Let's find out who did that shooting,' he said. Rachel sighed, then followed him as he heeled his mount down the slope in the direction from which the gunfire had sounded. They rode cautiously through the trees, Otis keeping the lead.

Fifteen minutes later, they heard a man's voice cursing over and over. Following on, they first spotted the head-shattered body of the Indian lying in a pool of blood — and then, drawn by the blaspheming, they came upon Will Selby, an arrow jutting from his thigh, his simian features twisted with pain. He was slumped down in the grassy nook, concentrating on his colourful language. But he quieted as he heard their approach, his head jerked up, his eyes widening with alarm in anticipation of facing more Indians, alarm that suddenly gave way to a gawk of utter disbelief. 'Lockhart! You're a damned . . . *ghost?*'

Otis shook his head.

'I . . . I thought you was dead and buried!' Selby spluttered.

Otis gazed at him, realizing that he was one of his former companions, yet not knowing which one, the face with its jutting brow-ridges and heavy jaw being totally unfamiliar, yet possessing the capacity to make him uneasy. 'Where's

145

your partner?' he asked.

'How come you're alive?' Selby persisted, still unable to believe his eyes. He shifted slightly, grunting as the pain caught him, then gasping, 'Got to get this damned arrow out.'

'Where's your partner?' Otis repeated.

'Willoughby's dead,' Selby responded. 'Killed by that red-belly over there. Guess he won't do no more killin', but I sure hope he ain't got no pals around.' He met Otis's eyes, then said, 'Willoughby told me you'd died, that he'd filled in your grave . . . '

'Well, I guess he made a poor job of filling in — and I'm mighty sure I'm not dead. It seems a bullet caught me across the side of the skull. Can't remember a damned thing now.'

'Well I'll be . . . ' Selby's jaw sagged in bewilderment. He wondered if Willoughby might return to life in the same way, but dismissed the idea, never having found that miracles came in pairs. He noticed the girl for the first time. She gazed at the protruding arrow in awe, then she raised her blue eyes and nodded a greeting. God, she was pretty, with a woman's tits on a little girl's frame. Here he was with an arrow through his leg, out of his head with pain, and suddenly he was more concerned about what was beneath a female's skirt. He wondered if she was a virgin, or had Lockhart already inflicted his depravity on her?

'I'll see if I can get that arrow out,' Otis said.

8

It wasn't easy work, fixing Selby's leg. The arrow, a Juneberry shaft some twenty inches long with zigzag lines cut into it, had an iron tip which had penetrated so deep into his thigh, that its point had raised the skin three inches below his groin. But he'd been lucky. Further forward and the femur would have been shattered — slightly higher and his private parts would have suffered.

Rachel hurried away to the stream to fill their canteen; meanwhile Otis split Selby's trouser-leg. It would be impossible to pull the arrow out; it would have to be forced through. Selby lay back, his brow beading with sweat, his eyes streaming with pain. Using the knife which the Indian had discarded, Otis cut the shaft half way between its turkey-feather and its point of entry into the flesh. 'This might hurt a little,' he told Selby. 'Think of something good — like all that cash waiting up there in the cave.'

Momentarily, thoughts of the cash had faded from Selby's mind. Instead he had watched the slim back of the girl as she moved away, sworn to himself that if he survived this surgery, he would have her, no matter if he had to kill Lockhart to achieve it.

Meanwhile Rachel stooped at the stream, temporarily out of view of the others. She allowed the clear water to burble into the canteen. Once full, she corked it up. Her hands were shaking. Selby, even in his wounded condition, had disturbed her in a way she couldn't explain, making her innards pound. His eyes had lingered on her, as if he was stripping her naked in his mind. She forced her attention on to different matters. She figured Otis would need a strip of her petticoat, otherwise he'd never staunch the blood. If the wound went bad, his patient might lose his leg or even die, although she had heard that festering didn't come so quick in this high country. She rose to her feet, was returning, when Selby's hoarse scream startled her. Otis had extracted the red-shiny shaft, was holding it up like an accomplished sawbones. Selby was writhing on the ground, turning the air blue, while blood pumped from his thigh.

Rachel immediately tore a strip from her petticoat and she helped Otis bind it round to form a tourniquet. As the flow of blood diminished, they fastened a bandage over the entrance and exit holes made by the arrow and gradually Selby ceased his complaining, lapsing into a stupor. Otis washed the blood off the leg as best he could, after which he drew the trouser-leg together.

Rachel stood back, her face pale. 'I ain't never seen a man's pecker before,' she said, 'not close up like that, not even Jacob's.'

Otis raised his eyebrows in surprise. 'Were you impressed?'

'No, disappointed!'

They decided to stay in their present position for a while. They were both weary, as were their horses. Furthermore, Selby, currently snoring, was in no condition for travel, although he appeared to be showing no sign of fever.

Otis advised the girl to get some rest. She nodded, and as she found a comfortable spot, he dragged the dead Indian into some rocks where he would be out of sight to all except the overhead buzzards. He removed the remaining arrows from their quiver and broke them across his knee. At least that would prevent them from being used if they fell into Sioux hands again. He slackened the girths on the three horses — the two animals on which he and Rachel had escaped and the dun horse which had belonged to the Mexican bounty hunter. He left them grazing, then he climbed to the crest, sensing that this was the place from which Running Elk had launched his attack. He glanced around, fearful that more

Indians might appear, but the land showed no movement beneath the dull sky. He hunkered down, cradling the carbine, his eyes alert despite his tiredness.

He couldn't understand how he'd come to be half buried in his grave and somehow survived to find his way out of the hills, but he gave up trying to puzzle it out. There was so much where his brain had failed him. Maybe Selby, when he recovered from his ordeal, would fill in the gap, although Otis did not trust the man. At present, however, Selby would need their help, especially if his wound didn't heal. The fact that they had horses and food was also a reason for their companionship being welcome, particularly if they reached the cave and there was a heavy load of dollar bills to be conveyed. Also of value to Selby would be their ability to share in vigilance.

By evening, the patient was sitting up looking much brighter. He tucked heartily into the pemmican. Afterwards he suggested they moved on first thing in the morning. Otis nodded his agreement.

'How come you found yourself a pretty little female like her?' Selby enquired.

Rachel smiled, seldom before having been favoured with flattering comments.

'I picked her up in Heaven just before I came back to life,' Otis volunteered.

Selby grinned. 'I been thinkin', Lockhart. I'll keep watch for a while. You get some shut-eye. If any damned Injuns come chargin' over that crest, I'll give you a call.'

Rachel said, 'You sure need rest, Johnny No Name.'

Selby gave her an amused look. 'Johnny No Name, eh? He's got a name all right; Otis Lockhart, and it's known by every lawman and bounty hunter in the territory, same as mine.'

Otis ignored the comment. Rachel was right; he needed sleep, but his distrust of Selby was deepening by the minute. He wondered if he should have left that arrow in him to keep him subdued.

'Wake me up in a couple of hours,' he eventually decided. He lay back on the grass, pulling his battered hat over his face. He kept his eyes open for a long while, listening, hearing the dull thud of rain hitting the ground as the clouds at last opened up. Presently he dozed.

Dusk was thickening as Selby called to the girl, keeping his voice low so as not to disturb Lockhart. 'Wish you could slacken off this bandage. It's so tight it's hurtin'.'

Rachel had been sitting with her back against a boulder, her head drooping as weariness got the upper hand. She was awake instantly, the meaning of the words sinking in. She glanced at Otis. The hat still concealed his face but she noticed the easy rhythm of his breathing. Her eyes swung to Selby. He was sitting up, his coarse-featured face creased with the discomfort of his leg. She climbed to her feet and said, 'I'll tear off another bandage.' She hoisted

154

her skirt, ripping a further strip from her already ragged petticoat, unmindful of the low growl that the sight of her legs brought to Selby's throat.

'I best attend to it,' Otis said, removing the hat from his face and scrambling up. 'I must've had some medical experience. It comes kind of natural to me.'

The two men exchanged glares, neither fooled by the other's words.

'Keep your hands off Rachel,' Otis warned.

Selby glowered. 'You're a fine one to talk, Otis Lockhart. I ain't never been convicted for rapin' females!'

★ ★ ★

It was early afternoon of the following day and the weather remained dull and wet. Holy Jack and Jacob had kept to the high ridges and now they had reined-in at a point where the view was good. The old man was gazing through his eye-glass at the long, narrow valley to their left. Jacob was more concerned with the sickly smell that emanated from the sack tied across his father's saddle, obliging him to keep his distance. Holy Jack seemed untroubled by the stench, only occasionally waving his hand to drive the flies off, but the thought of the head with its sightless eyes and sagging, putrefying flesh made Jacob want to puke. If the law desired that grisly trophy, they were welcome to it.

'The Lord's name be praised!' Holy Jack suddenly exclaimed. 'My prayers have been answered, no mistake. And all the eggs in one basket.'

'What you s-seen, Pa?'

'Open your eyes, boy.' The old man was pointing. He held out the eye-glass which Jacob took, lifting it to scan the valley and discover the cause of his father's excitement. Three riders were strung out in single-file, still some way off but recognizable even so. Otis Lockhart, Rachel and a third man, undoubtedly the other escaped convict.

Jacob gave his father a withering look and said, 'You g-got more k-killin' in mind?'

Holy Jack shook his head. 'Killin', right now, would be wicked. Shots would stir up attention if any heathen ears are around. The good Lord has whispered to me, Jacob. He mentioned the word 'forgiveness'. To err is human, to forgive divine. Anyway, there's three of them to two of us, and we need them to lead us to the cash, remember? We'll join up with them, remind Rachel that she has a good home to return to, and we'll renew our friendship with Otis Lockhart.'

Jacob unleashed a scornful snort. 'I g-guess they'll hardly welcome us with open arms. Most likely they'll start shootin' as soon as w-we come in range.'

'You're a poor judge of character, son. Rachel will never let them do that. For all her sins, we're still her kin and blood's thicker than water. She won't forget that.' He poked a grubby finger into his mouth, rubbed his painful

157

gums. 'Now listen tight to what I want you to do. You ride down and make contact with them. Tell them old Holy Jack's waitin' a half-mile up the trail to meet them and that he's real sorry Rachel ran away and he don't hold no grudge about it, but just wants to help her do what's best.'

'And how about L-Lockhart and Selby?' Jacob asked.

Holy Jack smiled craftily. 'Tell them all I want is to let bygones be bygones. Tell them that the Lord has spoken to me and said we all got to help each other in this unfriendly country.'

Jacob sat blinking at his father, making no effort to comply with the instructions. So I'm the one to risk a bullet if they don't care for our company, he thought.

'Get on, Son,' his father snapped. 'You act as if it was a punishment to ride down and say hello to your sister.'

At last Jacob nodded. Maybe if he warned them in advance, they'd have time to make a run for it if they wished.

All he hoped was that they wouldn't put him in the same category as the old man. He touched his heels to the flanks of his horse.

Holy Jack watched his son ride down the slope, then he kicked his own animal into motion, moving parallel to the valley, keeping out of view behind the ridge. He had said he would wait half a mile ahead of where Jacob would converge with Rachel and the two men, but now he had a better idea. He would take up position at a much nearer point — on the top of a small promontory that jutted into the valley. He would then be within rifle range of the fugitives. If they cut and ran on seeing Jacob, he'd shoot at least one of them down, most likely Lockhart. He fondled the sack that hung from his saddle-bag. Two heads, he smiled to himself, are better than one!

Drawing up level with the promontory, he dismounted, ground-tethered his horse and crept forward. A few minutes later, he was sprawled belly-flat

159

on the high rock, the butt of his twin-barrelled Remington nestled into his shoulder, his view of events in the valley unimpaired.

* ★ ★ ★ *

Otis was leading the way when sudden shock slammed through him. It was communicated to his sorrel which reared and neighed in fright. 'It's your pa!' he cried, struggling to control his mount. Fifty yards up the valley, a lone horsemen, his slouch hat pulled down, had edged clear of some boulders and had reined in, blocking the way.

Rachel came alongside Otis, gasping, 'No, it's Jacob.'

Selby joined them, drawing his pistol. 'I say let's shoot him and be done with it.'

The girl swung round angrily. 'No,' she said. 'He's my brother.'

Selby mumbled something but lowered his gun, his eyes wild with alarm. Otis debated his options, but with Jacob waving his arm in an apparent goodwill gesture and nudging his horse towards them, it was a question of gunning him down, taking flight or hearing what he had to say. He noticed how the boy's rifle remained sheathed in its scabbard.

'He'll not harm us, not Jacob,' Rachel breathed.

Selby was cursing, not liking the turn of events at all.

'Let's hear him out,' Otis said. Mistakenly he'd believed that they were clear of pursuit from Rachel's kin. He was irked at having been taken by surprise again, but God had clearly fashioned this terrain for the benefit of ambushers. Now, he glanced around anxiously, wondering if Jacob was operating alone. 'Where's your pa?' he asked, as the boy reached them and drew rein.

Jacob caught his sister's eye. 'You all r-right, Rachel?'

She nodded. 'Till now. Tell us where Pa is.'

He gestured up the valley. 'Says he'll

m-meet us half a mile from here. He t-told me to let you know he don't bear no g-grudge for what's happened, that he's spoken with the Lord who t-told him, 'To err is human, to forgive d-divine'. Pa asked me to say he wants to let bygones be bygones.'

Otis hesitated. He sensed that Jacob was made of different stuff from his father, despite their similar looks. 'Can we trust him?' he asked.

Jacob didn't get the opportunity to set his stammering tongue in motion again. Selby cut in, 'If we ride on, he'll probably gun us down.'

'He w-wont do that,' Jacob managed.

Otis figured the boy was right. Surely the old man wouldn't open fire with his daughter and son in the firing zone . . . or would he? On the other hand, his offer of friendship might be genuine. Otis doubted this.

As for Will Selby, he had no such considerations. He made his mind up quite suddenly, slamming his good heel hard into the flank of the dun horse, wheeling it sharply across the valley floor. He'd gone scarcely ten yards before Holy Jack blasted off from his higher vantage point, his bullet driving into the lungs of the racing mount, pitching beast and rider over in a flurry of hooves and lather. Somehow Selby scrambled clear, attempted to run on, but his leg gave out and he went down and lay unmoving. Behind him, the dun horse flailed with its hooves in a vain attempt to cling to life.

Otis and Rachel had watched, the sheer speed of events stunning them. Simultaneously, Holy Jack was clambering down from his vantage point, his Remington levelled at them. Otis reached for his own gun, but Rachel grabbed his arm. 'Been enough killin',' she cried.

The old man stopped within a few yards then, without warnings, his wizened face split into a toothy smile. 'Well, it's sure good to see you, Rachel. Like Jacob told you, all I want is to make sure you're all right, to tell you that all is forgiven.'

'Then why're you pointin' that gun at us?' Rachel demanded, fury smouldering in her eyes.

'Because I gotta make certain you *want* forgiveness.' Holy Jack hesitated, then he reluctantly lowered the weapon. 'I guess now we're all friendly, there'll be no need for guns.'

'Pa!' Jacob cried, waving towards the fallen Selby. 'That fella's t-tryin' to get up!'

Holy Jack's face resumed its muskrat expression. 'Tie the bastard up. If he tries escapin', shoot him dead . . . but not in the head.'

9

Still dazed, Selby looked anxiously around in an unsuccessful effort to locate the pistol which had fallen from his grasp, then his gaze swung to the approaching Jacob and the gun he held levelled at him. Seeing that he had no alternative, Selby raised his hands, the hateful look on his face registering the disgust he felt at the turn of events. Jacob gestured with his gun and said, 'G-get back to the others!'

'I can't walk,' Selby gasped. 'My leg's busted.'

'Then crawl,' Jacob shouted, without trace of his stammer.

Selby swore, but then grimacing with pain, he hobbled to where Otis, Rachel and Jack waited. Jack had his Remington raised again, his finger flexing on the trigger. 'Tie him up, real tight,' he instructed his son. 'If he tries runnin' off again, we won't treat him so kindly.'

The boy did as he was told, roping Selby's arms and legs together. The outlaw fell to blaspheming and Holy Jack took offence, firing off his gun in anger. Selby immediately fell, not realizing that the bullet had been directed past him. His cursing had been stifled and, as he cottoned on to the fact that he was still alive, he pushed himself into a sitting position. 'My leg hurts like h — awful bad,' he complained.

The old man showed remarkable sympathy. 'That's why we tied you up. The rope'll act like a splint!' He slipped another shell into his gun. 'Now maybe we can talk turkey. I know what you're up to, headin' for where that loot is hid. If you wanna keep breathin', you best lead us there, then we'll have a share out and go our separate ways.'

Had Selby's eyes been bullets, Holy Jack would have gone down, riddled a thousand times over. Instead, all the outlaw could do was ask, 'How can I travel, tied up and crippled the way I am?'

'There'll be a horse for you to ride.'

Otis had been watching, not deceived by Selby's temporary helplessness. Without doubt he'd had a rough time, what with his arrow wound and tumbling from his horse, but right now he was playing his cards for all they were worth. With a constitution akin to that of a mountain grizzly, he would revert to form as soon as he got half a chance, and then somebody else would pay — heavily.

'Let's move out,' Jack said. 'All that shootin' will most likely have the entire Sioux nation lookin' for us!'

Selby's gaze lashed around the group and settled on Otis. 'Probably in league with the old man!' he snarled accusingly.

Otis shook his head, thinking I'd sooner be in league with a damned rattlesnake — but he said nothing. He in no way regretted that Selby had been tied up. He had seen him as a threat right from the time Rachel and he had found him, although now he felt somewhat sore that all the effort he had made to patch up the man's wound had been negated. Again, he reckoned that he should have let him bleed to death.

Rachel had remained quiet, misery stamped across her face; her eyes frequently darted to Otis as if for guidance — yet she had prevented him from drawing his gun earlier. Now Holy Jack, his Remington still ready in his hands, swung his attention to Otis. 'I guess you know the route to the cash after all, Lockhart?'

'He sure does, Pa,' Rachel cut in. 'He was takin' me to it.'

Otis responded to the desperation that flared in the girl's eyes and kept silent.

Holy Jack looked at Otis, his expression reflecting a new glimmer of interest.

Afterwards Otis realized why Rachel had spoken for him. If Jack believed that he, Otis, knew the location of the loot, it might restrain the old man from murdering him — unless his temper got the upper hand. He was no doubt reasoning that in the possible event of Selby succumbing to his wounds, Otis would prove an insurance. But from what Selby had said earlier that morning, they were now no more than a day's travel to the cache, and he had the feeling that everything would change once they reached that goal. All considerations were therefore short term.

'Rachel.' The old man gave his daughter a doleful stare. 'You been awful sinful, but I trust you've now seen the wickedness of your ways and your heart is full of repentance for leavin' your poor old father and brother to fend for themselves. The Lord has told me that if you take the righteous path from now on, He'll not hold what you done against you. Do you understand, Daughter?'

In a flat voice, Rachel said, 'I understand, Pa.' Then, with considerably more feeling, she added, 'But I love Otis, nothin' will change that!'

Her father scowled though he did not

enlarge upon the subject. Instead he levelled his gun at Otis and said, 'I figure, after the way you corrupted my innocent daughter, you best show a little goodwill and give back the gun you stole from my home.' He gestured to his son. 'Jacob, relieve Mister Lockhart of the hardware!'

Otis hesitated, but Rachel said in a resigned voice, 'Give it back. It's his gun anyway.'

Otis watched as Jacob stepped across and slid the carbine from its saddle scabbard.

'Now, Mister Lockhart,' Holy Jack went on, 'get off that horse so Jacob can fasten your hands behind your back.'

'Pa, there's no need . . .' Rachel cried out.

'Shut your mouth,' Jack shouted, levelling his Remington at Otis.

Otis had no desire to stir up more bullets, so he slid from his saddle and allowed Jacob to tie his hands. Simultaneously, Rachel whispered, 'Not too tight!' and Otis was aware that her

170

brother, surprisingly, heeded the advice.

'Let's move out,' the old man commanded. 'All the disturbance will most likely have the red heathens lookin' for us!'

Jack sent his son scurrying away to retrieve his horse, and on his return they organized their travel arrangements. There were now four animals between five people. Selby, complaining vociferously, was hoisted on to the sorrel that Otis had been riding, his feet fastened beneath its belly. Jack would lead the horse, clearly relying on Selby to point the direction. Jacob, obeying his father's orders, forced Otis to mount up behind Rachel, after which he linked his ankles with a rope in the same fashion as those of Selby, then he climbed into his own saddle. Once matters were arranged to the old man's satisfaction, they started on.

The only evidence of the drama that had occurred in that valley, at least to the untrained beholder, was the lifeless dun horse. It lay with one eye open, staring reproachfully at the sky. Already it was attracting the attention of buzzards and flies.

* * *

The light had faded and heavy spots of rain were falling, soaking the small cavalcade of riders and animals. Otis was biding his time, having no intention of remaining a prisoner indefinitely. The real crunch would come when they eventually reached the cash. That would be when Holy Jack ceased his mealy-mouthed talk of forgiveness. That was when Selby would stop any play-acting. Each man was as dangerous as the other. Each was consumed by greed and would stop at nothing to gratify it. There was sure to be some sort of showdown. At the moment, the old man was calling the tune but fortunes could change at any time. Jacob was an unknown quantity, quiet most of the time, yet Otis sensed that resentment against his father was hidden inside him like a snake's venom.

Rachel leaned her back into him as they rode, her head beneath his chin, the smell of her hair in his nostrils. With her skirt drawn up, her smooth, bare legs dangled down in front of his own. When he kissed the nape of her neck she groaned with ecstasy. He was certain she had not given up hope of escaping from the old man but, like Otis, she was biding her time. After all, each one of them was heading for the same place. There was no point in running off only to meet up again. The hidden cash was beckoning them like a finger.

Otis tried to form a plan. The girl's idea of travelling north into the obscurity of Canada, was immensely attractive. Once again he reminded himself that she was right: they needed money if they were to get clear away. There was no doubt that she intended to stay with him, and the thought of this warmed him. Maybe one day, if she came into contact with youngsters her own age, she would tire of him — but somehow he doubted it. She was in no ways fickle, though with the sap of youth hot inside her, she was hungry for experience. Again he thought how incredible it was that a vicious and cruel man like Jack should have sired a sweet-natured offspring — but maybe he hadn't. Perhaps Rachel had grown up misinformed of her parentage. After all, she was amazingly naive about life.

They progressed, the hills dark and brooding about them. The high crags loomed through the rain-mist. Selby indicated the route with an occasional mumbled and seemingly resigned word. Presently, Otis heard him question the old man. 'What you got in that sack that attracts so many flies? It stinks awful.'

Jack cleared his throat and spat. 'Meat. Ain't no need to concern yourself.'

Selby nodded and rode on, his head slumped down. Presently he complained, 'This damned rain. It's shrunk the rope. It's nigh stranglin' me!'

Jack made no response and Selby's head dropped lower against the neck of his horse.

'He looks downright sickly,' Rachel whispered to Otis.

'I wouldn't trust him,' Otis murmured.

Something was troubling the girl. 'I don't think we're headin' the right way. Seems different from the map. Still, I'm not gettin' it out to check. If Pa knew I had it, he'd grab it like a shot.'

'I guess Selby knows the way well enough; maybe he's following a different route — unless he's playing some sort of trick.'

The night closed in; the temperature dropped; the rain grew harder.

Although his arms were fastened behind his back, Otis was thankful that his bonds had not been drawn uncomfortably tight. 'One thing's certain,' he remarked. 'We'll never trace the cave in the dark. We'll have to make camp and find it tomorrow.'

'And then what?'

'And then we'll reach the moment of truth, Rachel.'

She went quiet for a while, then she murmured, 'Johnny No Name.'

'Yup?'

'Whatever happens to us . . . I'll always love you.'

10

Holy Jack chose to stop in a grassy clearing rimmed by a high bank to the north and dipping down to a narrow, rushing stream to the south. A spruce tree had been felled by lightning, dragging ragged roots from the ground. It blocked the streamside and provided cover for their camp. The ankles of Otis and Selby were unlinked and they were allowed to dismount under the strict eye of Jacob who held his gun at the ready. Otis wondered which way the boy would turn when the final dice was thrown? Would any loyalty he had to his father remain firm?

Meanwhile, Jack had scraped out a small pit, and Rachel found some dry sticks and placed them ready. Her father fumbled with some lucifers and started a fire. Otis licked his lips. The old man had done them few favours — but at least he appeared to have provisions and the prospect of hot coffee and meat, albeit old, was tempting.

Selby had lapsed into sullen silence and Otis had no desire to stimulate conversation. He reckoned that with the weather so wet and miserable it was unlikely that marauding Sioux would molest them. Indians preferred sunshine and daylight for killing. If trouble erupted, it would most likely come from within their party.

Watched and watchful, they attended to their calls of nature, and Jacob unsaddled the horses and set them to graze. Jack forced Selby to a tree, made him sit with his legs around it while he refastened his ankles, after which he released his wrists, then retied them loosely in front of him so he could eat. The prospect of food had made Selby unusually compliant.

As the fire crackled into life, Jack went to his sack and withdrew a couple of rabbits he had killed the previous day. Otis noticed how the sack still contained some bulk and he concluded that perhaps a further rabbit was left for a later meal.

Rachel skinned the rabbits, using her father's knife then, without hesitation she walked across to Otis and cut the bonds that joined his wrists. Jacob made no attempt to stop her, but the old man, seeing what she had done, sprang towards them.

'Damn you, girl! What you playin' at?'

Rachel positioned herself firmly between him and Otis, blocking the way. Jack would have pushed her aside, but Otis was sick of his bullying manner. 'Let her alone, you stupid old fool!' he shouted. 'I got better things to do than run off right now — and I'm not contemplating murdering anyone, not unless I'm forced to!'

Holy Jack was stopped in his tracks, taken aback. Nobody had spoken to him like that in years. Before he could retaliate, Selby shouted, 'And how about me? I'm sick of these damned ropes. Unless you cut me loose, old

179

man, you can go find that cash by yourself!'

Jack's wizened face worked with emotion. He opened his mouth to speak, his gums showing up awfully inflamed, but he said nothing. Eventually, he shrugged his shoulders. 'After we've eaten,' he muttered. 'I'll cut you free then.'

With sticks, Rachel had fixed up a primitive spit over the fire and soon the rabbits were roasting. As the sizzling aroma spread, Otis felt his taste buds reacting. The rabbits were not large. Individual portions for five hungry people would hardly be satisfying. Even worse, when Jack eventually separated the pieces, burning his fingers as he did so, the meat seemed to have shrivelled considerably. Nonetheless, they all tucked in, other considerations temporarily giving way to the demands of their stomachs. Otis glanced at Rachel, seeing how her face was bathed orange by the glow of the fire, how it glinted on her teeth. Her cheeks were pink where the cool night air touched them and her eyes sparkled. Despite the ordeal she had suffered, she seemed prettier than ever — even as she sucked rabbit bones and her chin glistened with grease. She glanced up, caught his eye and smiled, and he smiled back and knew then that he loved her. Nothing would ever change that, not now.

Suddenly Jack unleashed a yell. He'd dropped the bone he'd been chewing, was grasping his jaw, his eyes glazed over with agony. 'Damnation!' he yelled. 'The pain . . .'

'Always s-said you should have had that tooth p-pulled out,' Jacob said.

'You do it then!'

'Can't, Pa. Ain't qualified.'

Otis felt a strange confidence inside him. 'I'll pull the tooth out for you, old man.'

Jacob nodded, grinning at his father's distress.

Otis said, 'I'll need some string — tough string.'

Jacob went to where his tack was

heaped, rummaged in his saddle-bag and produced what was required. Taking it, Otis told Jack to lie on his back which he did, albeit grudgingly, but he was desperate with the pain and opened his mouth. Otis grunted with distaste at the unwholesome sight. It was like gazing into the fiery maw of a volcano. He probed with his finger and located the offending fang.

'Keep your mouth wide,' he instructed. 'Don't want my fingers bitten off.'

Jack was in no position to argue. Otis slipped the string around the tooth. He then set his knee against the old man's chest and yanked with all his might. The tooth came out, Jack howling and spluttering, his face covered with blood.

'You best go down to the stream, wash out your mouth,' Otis said. He glanced at the long-rooted tooth, still dangling on its string like a lassooed dragon. It was a monster all right. It was a wonder half of the jaw hadn't come with it. Even so, Otis felt a pang of satisfaction at his work.

Jack scrambled up, cradling his jaw, groaning. He started down towards the stream, then turned back to gather up his Remington.

Selby had watched the surgery with interest, but as the patient moved off his thoughts reverted to his appetite. He glanced at Rachel and said, 'A tiny bit o' rabbit ain't hardly enough to satisfy a halfstarved man. If there's another rabbit in the old man's sack, I vote we get it roasted.'

Otis nodded. 'Sounds a good idea, Rachel.'

Rachel, herself still famished, had moved to where her father's saddle-bags were heaped. She'd picked up the sack before Jacob, seemingly mesmerized by Otis's dental skills, cottoned on to what was happening and cried out, 'No, Rachel!'

It was too late. The girl had reached into the sack and half dragged the contents out. She suddenly screamed. With horror stamped across her face, she dropped the bundle. She was standing upslope from the others and the result was alarming. Willoughby's head acquired a life of its own, seeming to leap from the sack and roll downward, bouncing over the bumps like a ball, coming to rest scant feet from Selby. Incredulous recognition dawned in him. '*Grinner!*' He unleashed a great roar, all at once fighting the ropes that fastened him to the tree. Sheer bull-strength would have torn him free, had not Holy Jack, hearing the commotion, turned back from his mouth-washing chores. As he rushed to the main group, his eyes focused on Willoughby's head, then switched to the struggling Selby, seeing how close he was to escaping his bonds. 'That head's mine!' Jack shrieked out. He brought up his Remington, his face working with a fury that blinded him to sanity. He fumbled with the breech, then he blasted off with both barrels.

In the confusion, Selby twisted sideways, somehow avoiding the deadly slam of lead. As his ropes at last gave way, he scrambled up, roaring out his hatred for the old man.

On instinct, Otis sprang forward and lashed out with his fist, catching Selby squarely on his monolithic jaw, dropping him like a felled ox. Jack, his face contorted, ploughed in, his hands clawing for the unconscious Selby's throat. But Otis grabbed his shoulders, swung him around, dumping him unceremoniously on the ground. Jack was up immediately, desperate to renew his attack, but suddenly Jacob's cry sounded.

'Rachel's been hit!'

Otis spun around in alarm, his gaze riveting to the spot where Jacob was crouched over the fallen girl. Even in the dim fireglow, Otis saw the blackness of blood staining her dress and despair cut through him. The boy cried out, 'Pa's shot bounced off a tree . . . caught her full on!'

Otis scrambled across, dropped to his knees beside her, hoping, praying, that she was still alive, hardly aware that the old man had followed him, standing behind, cursing over and over. The bullet had struck her high on the chest and as Otis touched her he felt the moist warmth.

Rachel opened her eyes, stared up at him. She raised her hand and he took it, feeling the weakness in her. Her lips moved and he leaned close, hearing words that reached his ears only. 'I love you, my Johnny No Name.'

Afterwards, he swore she smiled. Maybe he kissed her lips one final time, but all he could recall was how her hand gripped his, then went limp; how grief made him choke.

Suddenly the old man shouted, *Rachel!* as if commanding her back to life . . . and then his voice changed to a whimper. 'She ain't dead, is she? Please God no. I never meant . . . never meant . . . '

Jacob had risen from his crouching position, his breathing coming in great rasps, tears streaming down his cheeks, but his voice sounded firm as granite.

'You evil man. You hounded our poor ma to her grave; you strangled Charlie Casement; you shot old Elijah; you drove Rachel into runnin' away; you sliced off that dead man's head . . . and now you've killed Rachel. My God, Pa, for all your pious preachin', you committed sins worse than anybody else on earth. You don't deserve nothin' but the fires of Hell — *and that's where I'm sendin' you!*' He brought up his gun, laid its muzzle against the old man's skull. Holy Jack's eyes, great blood-shot orbs, pivoted towards his son. 'You ain't got the guts to kill me, boy!'

Jacob pulled the trigger.

Entwined with the shattering reverberation of the blast, Otis's brain somehow registered that the boy had spoken without a single stutter.

All at once there was another sound — the thud of hooves from across the night-shrouded meadow. Will Selby had recovered his senses, had run off, but Otis was beyond caring. His sweet Rachel, a moment ago vibrant with life, was gone. So was her demonic father. He couldn't believe it.

* * *

There was no talk between them. Each was steeped in his own contemplations. Otis sat in vigil, close to her body, through the dark, drizzling hours, making no attempt to rekindle the fire as it died down. Jacob had dragged the old man's corpse off to the side, as if its very nearness was abhorrent. Presently he hunkered down beside Otis. At long last the heartless dawn probed cold light into the eastern sky, stirring the forest awake. Only then did the mourners start scraping at the soil, using gun-butts and hands, thankful for the rich softness of the earth. They toiled openly, not caring about Indians or any other enemies, their work taking precedence over all else. They fashioned Rachel's grave close to where she had fallen, doing their best to make it worthy of her, placing her deep enough to be safe

188

from scavengers. By the time they had finished, the sun had risen, the rain clouds gone.

Jacob now broke his silence, speaking prayers while they stood with their heads bowed. *Earth to earth, ashes to ashes.* . . . His stammer was gone.

Holy Jack was buried twenty yards away, back in a thicket and nowhere near so deep. If the wolves wanted to dig him up and wrangle over his bones, skin and straggly hair, they could do so. Afterwards, Otis consigned Willoughby's head to a hole midway between the two graves, glad to have its ugliness out of sight; he had no recollection of the man when he had been alive.

Then, for the first time, Otis caught Jacob's eye and he said, 'I guess you loved your sister.'

The boy nodded. 'Maybe I didn't realize how much I loved her till now. Mister Lockhart . . . did you do all those bad things? Hurtin' and killin' women, I mean?'

Anguish creased Otis's face. He

hesitated, finally said, 'I guess I did. I don't know what made me do it, but I guess I did.'

'And did you do bad things with Rachel?'

Otis sighed deeply. She'd been begging him to do 'bad things' with her . . . to show her what happened between men and women . . . the sins of the flesh. And he'd done nothing.

He hoped she'd find the sins she longed for in Heaven.

'No, Jacob,' he said. 'All Rachel and I did was to love each other.'

The boy nodded glumly. 'I'm goin' back, Mister Lockhart, back home. I don't want that cash. I don't want no more to do with this business.'

Otis extended his hand. They shook, then the boy went to his tack and lugged it over to the meadow. He saddled his horse, mounted up and rode down the slope not looking back.

Otis spent a further hour, fashioning a cross. When it was finished, he marked her grave, stood to gaze at it for a while, then he cleared up as much evidence as he could of the campsite, saddled both the remaining horses and mounted up. He struck out, having no idea of what he would do, where he would go. His brain seemed to have gone numb.

★ ★ ★

The following morning, Jacob stumbled across another campsite, now deserted but where the ashes of the fire and the horseshit were still warm. Jacob figured that at least a half-dozen men had spent the night here . . . and instinctively he knew it was Sheriff Rainbird and his posse, still intent on hounding escaped convicts. But now it was no longer his concern.

11

'Lockhart!'

The shout cut through the morning hush, snapped Otis from his melancholy. He jerked upright in his saddle, whipping the pistol out of his waistband, his eyes immediately drawn to the figure perched on a rocky outcrop twenty yards ahead of him.

The sun had risen brightly, but now as Otis had got closer to the towering crags, the air was cooling. He'd had little notion of where he was going, apart from the fact that he still hoped that across the border in Canada he might find some sort of sanctuary . . . and Canada lay to the north, beyond the barrier of the crags, beyond the great prairie that stretched for miles, without peak or mesa, empty as a dry sky. But his mind was dulled by grief. When he closed his eyes, he saw her lips, her smile; he heard her laugh, felt her touch and her name whispered to his lips. And he had ridden openly, leading the second horse on a hackamore rope, not caring over-much whether all the Indians, lawmen and bounty hunters in creation suddenly ambushed him.

Yet now the old instincts of preservation sharpened his senses because Will Selby was hobbling down from his rock, approaching him — and Will Selby was somebody Otis would never trust.

'You can put your gun away,' Selby called. 'You might have killed women, but you ain't the sort to shoot an unarmed man.'

The big Southerner looked played out, his apelike face still twisted with the pain of his leg . . . but sure enough he had no weapon. Clearly he hadn't had time when he took flight to do anything but leap astride a horse and ride. Otis lowered his pistol.

'Where's the others?' Selby enquired.

'You know about Rachel,' Otis said. 'After she died, Jacob shot his old man, then rode out.'

'Jesus Christ!' Selby exclaimed. 'I was plannin' to kill the old man myself. I wanted to strangle him with my bare hands, watch his eyes bulge. That's what he deserved, hackin' off Grinner's head and all.' He shook his own head as if to clear his mind of the thought, then he looked at Otis. 'Sure sorry about the girl. She deserved a good man. So it's just you and me left now, Lockhart. I guess we need each other. You got guns, saddles, horses, and I got cash — leastways I know where it's hid. Maybe we can work together, eh? Grinner and me always figured we'd go to South America, start a new life. Maybe me and you . . .'

'How do I know you won't shoot me down first opportunity?' Otis asked.

A smile curled Selby's lip. 'You got my word. I reckon it's time we applied a little of that 'honour among thieves' stuff.'

'You're not exactly a man of honour,' Otis said.

'And neither are you, Otis Lockhart.'
The words stung Otis but he had no answer.

'Have you got any eats?' Selby asked. 'I'm down-right sick of huckleberries. I'm starvin'.'

Otis nodded. 'I got some dry rations, courtesy of Holy Jack.'

Selby's smile widened. His mouth was watering at the prospect of food. His eyes hovered over the saddled horse, the guns. 'Thank God I won't have to ride bare-back any longer,' he said. 'When we've eaten, we'll go on to the cave, get those sweet dollar bills loaded up. Maybe we'll rest for a day or so, then we'll quit these doggone hills for ever.'

Otis decided to take Selby at his word. Maybe he was being foolish, but he felt too weary for further conflict. Selby was in no fit condition to control animals and to load the heavy wads of cash on to their backs. He required all the assistance he could get. Maybe he'd meant it when he'd said they needed each other.

'Food,' Selby reminded Otis.

Otis nodded, went to the old man's saddle-bags and shortly afterwards they were munching on hardtack, brown bread which was even harder, and dried entrails. 'Sure would welcome some fresh meat,' Selby commented, wiping his hands on his shirt. 'When we reach the cave, we can set snares.'

'How long will it take us from here?' Otis enquired.

'Couple o' hours, no more. Then we'll be real wealthy men, Otis Lockhart. And we can have all the fillies we want. Say, I been thinkin': what with havin' all those guns from Holy Jack, you got more'n you need. You never know when a war party of red-bellies may come chargin' over the ridge. A man needs to defend hisself. Just let me have a pistol . . . and maybe Jack's old Remington.'

'The Remington!' Otis exclaimed. 'That was the gun which killed Rachel.'

'I know,' Selby responded. 'That's why I figured I should have that

196

weapon, so's it wouldn't keep remindin' you of what happened.'

Otis nodded reluctantly.

Within an hour they were on the move again, Selby having recovered his own horse from a nearby thicket. Now armed, he rode ahead, leading the way. Otis watched him like a hawk, ensuring that his own pistol was loaded and at hand. As they climbed higher, moving through yellow pine and gnarled red cedar, their horses were slowed by the steep ground.

★　★　★

They were in the shadow of two great peaks when Selby pointed excitedly. 'See them trees, all spread out in a line, like a troop of cavalry on the charge? The cave's in that ravine down on the left.' He glanced over his shoulder, his face exultant. 'We made it, Otis!'

They negotiated a narrow ridge, then set their animals up a rocky gradient. Otis scanned the granite face along the ravine side but saw no sign of an opening. 'If you didn't know it was here,' Selby explained, 'you'd ride straight by.'

Otis said, 'How come you found it in the first place?'

'A fella we had in the gang was half Sioux. He knew about it, figured it'd be the perfect place to hide the cash.'

'So there's others around who know where the cash is?' Otis enquired.

Selby shook his head. 'All killed, even Charlie Casement.' He didn't enlarge upon the matter and Otis felt disinclined to press him.

Five minutes later, having left their horses tethered to boulders under a traprock shelf, they reached a narrow fissure in the rock wall. Selby had found a dry clump of wood. Otis scraped a match and ignited the clump. With the light, they went through the opening.

The cave was surprisingly big and the air was rank with a thick redolence. 'Bear smell,' Otis whispered. 'Bear must've used this place.'

Selby laughed. 'Must be the richest bear in the whole world.'

Otis nodded. He'd never seen Selby in such good spirits. He figured that far back there must be another entrance big enough for a bear to use. Please God, he thought, may that critter not be at home!

Selby raised the torch, setting shadows dancing along walls which were pocked with hollows and slits. Otis glanced around, awed by this convoluted place, conscious of the raised hairs on his nape, conscious that he and Selby were intruding into somewhere which had slumbered, disturbed only rarely, for millions of years.

The cave curved and twisted like a maze, its floor strewn with a jumble of boulders over which they scrambled. Selby seemed to have forgotten about his wounded leg; his speed quickened with every step. Above their heads, daggers of feldspar jutted downward.

They came to a natural archway, shaped like a cupola, twelve feet across.

This led into a further gloomy chamber, and suddenly Otis noticed a freshness in the air, proving that, as he'd supposed, there was another opening to the outside world further on.

'See, against the wall,' Selby exclaimed, 'there's a hole that leads into a deep pit. The cash is there. Won't be no problem, scramblin' down.'

Otis could see no indication of any hole. They moved closer, stooped down and only then did he see a black gash close to the rock wall. It was mostly hidden by the unevenness of the floor. He wondered if there might be snakes down there, entwining themselves in all that money.

All at once the torch flickered out and they both cursed. Then Selby laughed. 'Always was kinda creepy, this place. This wood ain't gonna burn no more. You best go and find another clump, then come back and I'll go down and start liftin' out the cash. My God, I sweated them prison years, just dreamin' of this moment.'

'I'll be back soon,' Otis said, and then he back-tracked, praying he wouldn't get lost now that he was groping along in darkness. Once, he caught his head on a rocky outjut. He stopped for a moment, but when the dizziness cleared he pressed on. Five minutes later he encountered a glimmer of light which strengthened as he progressed.

When he emerged into the sunshine, it took him a while to locate a suitable piece of wood, but he eventually found a twist of vine which he felt would serve the purpose. As he was scrambling back towards the cave entrance, he became aware of the horses, tethered beneath the traprock shelf. They were blowing and prancing, their shod hooves noisy on the shale. Something had spooked them. He paused, feeling uneasy. After a while they quieted. He climbed to the ridge and peered down the craggy slope over the way they had come, shading his eyes against the sun. There was no movement down there, no birds, no chipmunks, nothing. He went to the horses. They were still jittery, their nostrils fluttering. Maybe a snake or wolf had startled them. Or had they scented something on the air, like the odour of Indians? He soothed them. He waited. Nothing untoward showed so, only partially satisfied, he retraced his steps to the cave.

Ten minutes later, he went through the archway and called to Selby, thankful for his irritated response: 'Where the hell d'you get to!'

With light restored, Selby made his descent, disappearing into the depths. Otis waited, crouching down, knowing that if he chose, he could roll a boulder across, seal off the hole and be rid of Selby for good. He shrugged off the thought. He wondered whether that bear might come lumbering along to investigate what was happening . . . and then, inevitably, his thoughts swung to Rachel. If, as she'd wished, they could just have had a little of that money and escaped together . . . He drew a deep, shuddering breath . . . *if only*.

Suddenly an anguished cry erupted from the depths. Otis straightened up in alarm, figuring Selby must have thrust his hand into a nest of snakes. The light flared as he reappeared, clambering from the hole — and in that flickering flame his primeval face was gnarled with anguish. He tried to speak, couldn't. He kept moving his head from side to side as if striving to shake off a nightmare — but it wasn't snakes which had distressed him. 'All gone,' he finally croaked. '*Every last dollar's gone!*'

* * *

Sheriff Fred Rainbird and his posse of seven deputies from Horn Ridge Springs were anxious to bring their manhunt to a conclusion. They were tired of slinking through Indian country where they knew they were risking their scalps every minute, but the prospect of catching the convicts had lured them on. Strangely, it seemed the Indians had helped them. They had found

Willoughby's disturbed grave, seen how his corpse was skewered by an arrow. This was the first time Rainbird had known Indians to excise the entire head instead of just the scalp, but there was no accounting for taste. So their prey had diminished to two. By now, however, patience was wearing thin and their aim of taking the fugitives 'dead or alive' had narrowed down to 'dead'. And as the trail of the two men grew hot, they were determined to execute their task without delay.

Knowing they were closing on their prey, they had tethered their horses in some trees and crept forward to a low ridge. From this, they were afforded a good view. They had seen Otis Lockhart emerge from the ravine and search for his stick of dry timber. Rainbird had no idea where he'd appeared from, but he felt sure the second man, Selby, would be hidden there somewhere. It annoyed Rainbird that the convicts' horses had picked up the scent of their own mounts and had started their racket, but it couldn't be helped.

With a grunt of anticipation, young Deputy Tresslock raised his rifle to his shoulder and settled his sights on Lockhart, intent on completing at least part of the mission, but before his finger could tighten on the trigger, Rainbird hissed, 'Don't be a fool! Hold your fire.'

Tresslock lowered his gun, his young eyes blazing with frustration. 'I could've got him.'

The old scar on Rainbird's cheek had reddened. It always did when he felt he was dealing with simpletons. 'There's two of them. They're bound to come for their hosses sooner or later. If we start shootin' now, we'd get Lockhart for sure, but the other fella would most likely run off. If we bide our time we can get 'em both.'

Tresslock grudgingly nodded his understanding, then he covered his humiliation with a show of renewed confidence. 'When those two fellas come for their horses, we'll fill 'em so full o' holes they won't make no shadow, eh?'

Rainbird turned to his other deputies, ordering them to make certain they stayed out of sight, and not to open fire until both men appeared *together*. They all agreed this made sense. A volley of well-aimed shots would be the quickest way of finishing this whole miserable business. Then they could go home. They settled down, concealed by the rocks, quietly checking their weapons.

The first man to keep watch was Harry Connell. He actually got Lockhart in his eye-glass, saw him quiet the horses, then disappear into the ravine. The sun had started into its westward drift.

Twenty minutes later, Rainbird muttered. 'Hope they don't slip away after dark.'

Harry Connell was about to express similar concern when he suddenly snapped to full alertness. 'No fear o' that, Sheriff. They're comin' out right now — both of 'em!'

Within seconds, the remaining posse were on their feet, lifting their guns to their shoulders.

★ ★ ★

Selby was swaying like a drunk as they quit the cave into the slackening light of evening. The disappearance of the cash seemed to have turned his brain. Everything he'd dreamed of, worked for, killed for, all these years had been snatched away. And then realization dawned in him and he spat out the name, *'Charlie Casement — that slippery bastard must've moved it!'*

Otis, following a yard behind his companion, had no time to comment; the murderous roar of rifle-fire curtailed all discussion.

12

It was as if the air was filled with hornets. In the maelstrom of bullets, both men fell behind the jumble of rocks, lost to the view of their attackers. Otis rolled until his back thumped against a boulder jarringly. The shooting had stopped, but through its distorting echo, he could hear men shouting, hear the crunch of boots as they hurried up the intervening slope. He had been hit, badly. His chest felt as if it was encircled with a tight band, curbing his breathing, squeezing his blood out.

He raised his head, saw Selby sprawled ten feet away, half his skull blasted off. Otis forced himself into a sitting position, pain cutting him with the intensity of a white-hot wire. His mouth was flooded with blood. He spat it out. The footsteps were getting closer, along with the rasp of laboured breathing, of shouts. Any second, heads would appear over the lip of the ravine and he would be a sitting target. He had to move, no matter the pain. Gritting his teeth, he forced himself on to his feet, fighting the mists that swirled in his head. Clutching his side, his fingers slippery with blood, he ran for the only sanctuary available — the cave.

He reached the opening, thrust himself through as his enemies charged into the ravine, one of them shouting, 'Where's the other bastard!'

Otis didn't look back. He plunged deep into the blackness, scrambling across the jumble of boulders; all the bruising and bumping that his body took was dwarfed by the pain of his wound. He figured the bullet had caught him low in the chest. His breath was shallow and painful to draw, and his ribs felt as though they were on fire. He moved like a blind crab, thankful that he had covered this way four times already and no longer needed light.

But his strength was ebbing, weakness radiating from the agony in his chest. Was the bullet lodged inside him — or had it gone straight through?

He halted, restrained his wheezy breath, listened. He could hear rocks being dislodged and men calling to each other. They'd entered the cave, but he saw no evidence of light probing through the passageways. They wouldn't find him without a torch.

Wincing with pain, he pulled off his shirt, rolled it into a bundle and pressed it against his wound. The shirt was already sodden, but at least it might staunch further bleeding. His side felt as if it was stiffening. He gritted his teeth, started on again, but he knew he was incapable of going far. Shortly he realized he had passed through the natural archway and was in the chamber where the pit was — close to the left-hand wall. He also recalled that somewhere ahead must lie the other entrance to the cave. Frantically he debated which option to take — escape through the far opening or concealment in the pit. His failing strength made the decision for him. He dragged himself off to the left, fumbled with his hands along the wall and located the hole through which Selby had vanished earlier that afternoon — the hole where once a fortune in cash had been hidden. He lowered himself into it, discovered a series of ledges leading down, but he lost his grip and fell through the darkness. He thudded on to the rock floor, was stunned into oblivion.

* * *

The voice echoed weirdly from the chamber above. 'Come out, Lockhart. We know you're here. Give up now, and you'll get a fair trial.'

Like hell I will, he thought.

He was lying on his back. He felt as if a heavy iron bar was pressing on his chest. He wanted to groan, but he suffered in silence, hoping that the frantic beating of his heart didn't carry to those who hunted him. Dim light flickered downward and he could hear men moving about above him. If they discovered the opening to the pit, he would be utterly trapped. He closed his eyes, gritted his teeth, and prayed. He counted off the people who had died violently in this crazy venture — Grinner Willoughby, Holy Jack, Will Selby, the Mexican bounty hunter, and poor Rachel. Was he next on the list? All it needed, was for somebody to send light down into the pit, cry out that he was found, then the whole mob would pour lead into him. This time there would be no escape.

'Where are you, Lockhart! Damn you!' The voice was crazy mad, seeming directly over him. 'You're asking to be blasted out!' And with that a gun roared off in the cave, three quick shots, setting up an echoing cacophony of splintering rock as the lead ricocheted against the walls.

'Crazy son of a bitch!' somebody yelled. 'You gawn and shot me in the foot, you bastard!'

'God! I never meant to hit you, Harry. Just wanted to scare Lockhart, wherever he is.'

There was a great deal of scuffling above him, a lot of blaspheming and berating of somebody called Tresslock. Then Otis heard another voice. It seemed one of the men had gone further into the cave, but now had been brought back by the sound of the shots. After the turmoil had been explained, the newcomer spoke again, and Otis guessed it was the sheriff. 'There's another opening further along. I reckon that's where Lockhart has gone. He don't seem to be around here.'

'Unless he's died already.'

'I'll believe that when we find his body. Every second we waste here, he's most likely gettin' further away. Let's press on.'

'I can't walk on this damned foot,' the man called Harry complained.

'Give him a hand, somebody. Tresslock, you did it. Most likely only a rock ricochet anyway.'

Suddenly the light around Otis grew stronger. Somebody was holding a torch directly over the pit. 'Some sort o' hole here,' a voice said. 'Maybe he's down here.'

Another voice called, 'Well, put a shot or two down there. That'll settle things.'

Otis grew rigid, death was staring him in the eye.

'I ain't firin' off in this place. Just as likely bounce back at me.'

'Come on, Greg,' Otis heard Sheriff Rainbird call from further back. 'We sure wasted enough time in this stinkin' place.'

The light was withdrawn, plunging Otis into merciful gloom. Boots scraped on the rocks, men cursed as they stumbled. It seemed an age before their noise had faded. Only then did Otis exhale, never more thankful for utter, impenetrable blackness.

How long would it be before they returned?

He wondered how seriously he was

wounded. All he knew, was that he was hurting badly. Could be he would die anyway in this ready-made grave. His bundled shirt was stuck over the bullet hole. He figured the bleeding had stopped.

He would have welcomed sleep. He closed his eyes but forced them open again. He was sure that if he gave in, he might never wake up. He kept recalling how Johnny No Name had crawled from his grave in the first place, clawing his way back to life. It just didn't seem right that he should have gone to all that trouble so he could find another hole to die in. Yet what alternatives did he have?

He'd lost Rachel and the rest of his so-called friends. He was hundreds of miles from civilization where he was hated for his awful crimes and any welcome he might receive would be in the form of a lynch rope. He was lost in a wilderness and Indians would rip off his scalp at the first opportunity, and he was being hunted by Sheriff Rainbird and his mob who would shoot him on sight. Furthermore he was without a horse and weapons. Add all this to the fact that he was probably dying, here in a tomb-like cave, from this damned bullet wound.

In short, his prospects were not rosy.

His thoughts swung to Selby, the sight of him stepping before him from the cave, still stunned by the absence of the cash . . . and the final words he'd spoken: 'Charlie Casement'. And now an interesting possibility occurred to Otis. If Charlie Casement had been responsible for moving the money before his horrific demise at the hands of Holy Jack, the map he had given to Rachel most likely indicated the present location of the cash.

Rachel had, in fact, doubted that Selby was taking them to the spot the map indicated, though Otis had not paid much attention to her comments at the time. Casement's map had been in the pocket of the girl's dress when she had been buried. He sighed. What good could this surmising do him? He turned his mind back to his predicament.

He strove to find anything that offered him a chance of survival. It was possible that the posse had not seen him disappear into the cave, that it might have been some time before they discovered its existence. That being so, they may have had no positive knowledge that this was the way he had come.

Slim hope goaded him into action. His and Selby's animals might still be where they'd been tethered to the rocks. If not, Rainbird and his men had been on foot. That meant that their horses must have been left out there. Maybe somebody was guarding them, but that was a bridge he'd have to cross. He recalled how he'd acquired a mount from the Indians — Rachel's Appaloosa. Fate had smiled on him then, albeit in a mean sort of way. Once again, if he was astride a mount, his chances would be better. And maybe the gun he'd dropped when he'd been shot might still be waiting to be retrieved. God, he was sure due a helping of good luck! He wondered if he had the physical strength to struggle on. The spirit was willing, but would the flesh prove too weak?

He had no idea how long he had lain unconscious. Maybe it was dark outside. He hoped it was. Determined now to make his effort, he reached out in the darkness, his hands clawing over the rocks to find the wall of the pit. He succeeded, though his suffering and stiffness made him grunt. Ignore the pain, he told himself, ignore the damned pain. He concentrated on drawing air into his lungs, on loosening up his joints. He located the ledges, the handholds and footholds. He pushed himself upward, finding his grip. His body felt as if it weighed a ton, but he straightened up and using his knees, chin, elbows, feet and hands began his ascent. Five minutes later he was out of the pit.

He paused, crouching down in the darkness, recovering his strength, orientating himself. He knew Rainbird and his men might come blundering back into the cave, using it as a shortcut to return to their horses. Please God, no — not until I'm out of it. He could not afford to linger. He forced himself onto his feet, started forward. He went, doubled up with pain, concentrating on one step at a time. He had no concept of passing time. It could have been an eternity that he drove himself onward. But gradually he realized that he was winning his immediate battle. Several times he swore he heard some movement far behind him and this quickened his pace; his fears, for some reason, dwelling on the fact that the bear might be back in residence, picking up the unwelcome scent of intruders. At last, thin light appeared ahead of him. It brought him the satisfaction that he was nearing the cave's opening, and also the grim knowledge that he would not have the cover of darkness once he emerged into the ravine. The night had come and gone.

After his hours in darkness, the light seemed harsh. He crouched down just inside the opening and peered out. Sure enough, there was daylight out there. Not the stark brightness of the high sun, but the early, misty light of dawn. He couldn't stay where he was. If somebody was watching the cave with a gun in their hands, he would be an easy target. So be it. It was a risk he had to take. He sucked cold air into his lungs, and vacated the sanctuary of the cave.

No bullet greeted him.

He glanced around at the ridges, saw no movement. He edged to his left, striving to keep his boots from rattling the shale. He passed the place where Selby's body had been. It had been taken away; the rocks were still dark with his blood, a fact that a multitude of flies had already noted. Also gone was the gun Otis had dropped. Five minutes later he reached the spot beneath the traprock shelf and groaned. The only evidence that their horses had been here, were the scattered heaps of dung — all long steamed-out and cold. No doubt Rainbird had commandeered the animals.

Otis moved on, swallowing back his frustration. Once he froze in alarm as an ugly screech sounded. He glanced up, saw a turkey buzzard hovering in the sky, its bald snake-head peering down, seeking its breakfast. If only he could share the bird's view of the surrounding terrain.

He was debating whether or not to discard his original intention of getting to Rainbird's horses. He had no idea where they were, and anyway there was bound to be a guard with them. But then fate, contrary as ever, took a hand, for he heard equine blowing, an early frolicking, and it seemed like a sure-fire invitation to revert to his plan. He'd stolen a horse from under the eyes of enemies before. He could do it again. So he reasoned.

Easing his head carefully above the lip of the ravine, he gazed down the ridged slope to where the trees thickened. Clearly the remuda of posse mounts was concealed there. If he was to get to them, he had no option but to cross the intervening slope, exposing himself to anybody with a gun — if they were looking his way. Maybe they would not be. Maybe they would be too engrossed with attending to the horses, or fixing their own breakfast. The thought of food made him realize how hungry he was himself — but he had no time for such luxury now.

He tried to straighten up, but the pain in his chest kept him doubled. Even so, he hoisted himself out of the ravine and went forward, glancing desperately ahead, wondering, with each step, if it would be his last.

But he had momentarily overlooked the threat from behind him.

Young Tresslock, hurrying ahead of his companions as they returned through the cave, emerged from the ravine, his eyes immediately drawn to the figure moving down the slope. A grin widened his lips. My God, he thought, this time Rainbird won't stop me from gettin' that bastard.

Otis stumbled but struggled on, his breathing coming with the unevenness of a rusty saw. Even so, the slotting of metal on metal as Tresslock frantically cocked his weapon came crystal clear — the deadly warning that a shot was about to come. Otis ran, tensing himself for the impact of lead, throwing himself towards the trees.

Fifty yards behind, Tresslock gritted his teeth in the expectation of the coming blast, steadied himself, took careful aim and pressed the trigger. Instead of the ear-cracking detonation, there came the leaden, lifeless snap of a firing pin biting into a bad round, followed by the 'chock' of the bullet lodging midway in the barrel. The foul word Tresslock used carried equally clearly to Otis, as had the earlier metallic click. He ploughed on and made it to the concealment of the trees. His strength giving out, he collapsed face down amid ferns.

Back on the ridge, Tresslock had been

joined by Rainbird and the others. Rainbird glared at Tresslock, ignoring the young man's excuse of, 'That Lockhart is the luckiest devil I've ever known!'

The sheriff waved his men forward.

Otis raised his head, peered out into the strengthening daylight, saw the posse spreading wide in a sort of skirmish line — six men, all with guns in their hands, heading straight for him. If he'd had a Gatling gun he could have mowed the lot down in one clean sweep, but he had no such weapon, not even a pistol. His only defence was his legs, and they were failing fast. But fear gave him strength to scramble from the ferns and, like a desperate, wounded deer, he drove himself on through the forest, tangled branches and thorny growth snatching at his legs, bare torso and face.

They were gaining on him; he could hear their shouting and the wild swish of the undergrowth as they surged in his wake. He stumbled over a tree root, forced himself up, fell again. He could hear movement to his left and, rising once more, he veered to the right, scaring an elk from his path. He reached the fringe of the trees, saw a grassy sloping vale ahead and charged on, knowing he had to cross it to reach the next crest.

Scarcely was he out of the trees, when the pound of hooves sounded loudly in his ears and fleetingly he realized that he had overlooked the remuda of horses — and their possible guard. Too late, he tried to lunge away, but a big grey horse galloped right into him, bowling him over — rider and beast unable to take evasive action.

He was dimly aware of Rainbird's voice behind him, of men crowding around, of hooves pounding the ground, of the stark reality that he could run no more. He didn't care what happened to him. The dizziness that swirled in his head had turned to black unconsciousness. He was thus oblivious to the fact that it was not Rainbird's man who had run him down, but an army lieutenant.

13

In sending Custer's expedition to probe the Black Hills, the US Government had gone back on the basic agreement brokered in the 1868 Laramie Treaty — that the sacred area would remain Indian territory for all time, that no white man would set foot there other than by invitation. No such invitation had been sought nor given.

Officially, the aim of the expedition was to discover more about the aboriginal trails leading to the Missouri River agencies from the Yellowstone and to establish a satisfactory site for a fort. Unofficially, Custer's brief was to look for gold. The Indians, well aware of the invasion of their hills by the creaking, jingling train of canvas-topped wagons, were mightily displeased, but the strength and firepower of the huge column had deterred them from intervention.

Before dawn, on this July morning of 1874, Lieutenant Anson Crawford, a wiry, hard-bitten forty year old with a determined jaw, had led out his patrol to reconnoitre the anticipated route of the main column that day. Following his commander's example of leading from the front, it had been Crawford, astride his strong, leggy grey, who had run Otis down. The sudden thudding encounter with another human being, plus the realization that he appeared to be a white man, astonished the officer. Now, as he brought his mount under control and slid from the saddle, more men were appearing from the timber. Foremost among them was a scar-faced individual with a badge pinned to his brightly coloured vest. At this moment, the rest of the army patrol came pounding up, reining in their horses, as surprised by this confrontation as their commander.

Seeing that no danger was threatened by the civilian party and deciding that they were as they appeared to be, a posse of lawmen, the lieutenant knelt beside the unconscious man, seeing the blood on him.

The man with the star was struggling to recover his breath. 'I'm Sheriff Fred Rainbird from Horn Ridge Springs,' he panted. 'This fella's an escaped convict, a killer. I've a warrant for his arrest. He's due a hangin', I can tell you.'

Crawford had straightened up, frowning. The posse had no right to be in this country, whether they were pursuing a criminal or not, but neither did the army, so he didn't press the point. Instead, he said, 'He's not fit for hanging without seeing a doctor first. I'm taking him back to our main column so Doctor Fitzroy can patch him up, that's if he hasn't pegged out before we get there. I suggest you come along and explain things to the general.'

Rainbird wasn't happy at having the fugitive snatched from under his nose, nor were his men. He started to argue, but then trailed off, seeing that the lieutenant was determined to carry out

228

his intentions. The sheriff tried to reestablish some of his authority. 'This fella's as slippery as a damned snake. Unconscious or not, I want him cuffed.'

Crawford straightened up, resignedly nodding his agreement. 'As you wish.'

★ ★ ★

Otis could feel bumping. He groaned. A strong smell lingered in his nostrils. It was laudanum. He tried to raise his arm but something was restraining it at the wrist. He started to move his legs but desisted. His entire body hurt — but his chest was the worst. It felt as if somebody had been digging into it with a shovel. The bumping continued and he could hear the jingle of harness and the voices of men. Closer, he distinguished the rattle of what seemed like surgical instruments in a dish. Where's Rachel? he thought, then something clicked in his mind and grief, sour and pitiless, jabbed at him. By the time he got his eyes open, he'd realized he was

229

in a wagon. Sight of white canvas over his head confirmed that knowledge. It was a big wagon. His vision adjusted to his immediate surroundings and he found he was not alone. An impish face with chipped, green-coloured teeth, was thrust close. The face reminded him of an evil pixie. Its owner said, 'He's a-comin' round. Thought he'd never make it.'

Fingers touched his nose, feeling the kink where it had once been broken. They were not the fingers of the impish-faced pixie. 'It's him all right,' a deeper voice proclaimed.

'Otis Lockhart,' the pixie said. 'Seems dead funny, patchin' a fella up so's he's fit enough for hangin'. Still, after all the things he's done he can't expect nothin' else but the rope.'

Otis realized that his chest was heavily bandaged. 'Where am I?' he managed. 'My chest is . . . agony.'

The pixie said, 'Of course it is, after what we done to you. You're in an army ambulance, courtesy of the Seventh

Cavalry. Doc Fitzroy has just cut a bullet out from between your ribs. Lucky for you it didn't get your lungs.'

Otis noted how they were wearing army uniforms, the smaller impish-faced man having two chevrons on his sleeve. Fitzroy was bulky, had heavy burnsides and a moustache, his chin clean shaven. Both were steadying themselves against the bump of the wagon as it rolled over uneven ground. Otis suddenly recalled his frantic efforts to escape the posse. 'Where's those lawmen?' he asked.

This time it was Fitzroy who answered. 'Rainbird and the rest of his men are riding along with the column, kicking their heels until you're well enough for them to take custody of you.'

'When'll that be?'

'That's for the general to decide.'

Again, Otis tried to move his arm and failed. This time he discovered he was handcuffed to the iron bedstead on which he was lying. 'All these wicked crimes I've committed,' he murmured.

'Can't remember any of them.'

Corporal Pixie sniggered. 'Fine story!'

'It's true,' Otis insisted. 'Look on my head. There's a scar there where an Indian bullet caught me. Since then, I can't remember a thing about my past.'

The corporal scoffed dismissively, but Doctor Fitzroy fingered back Otis's hair and examined the scar. 'Shook your brain up, I guess,' he commented. 'Could be you're telling the truth. The condition is known as amnesia. Sometimes the memory returns, sometimes it doesn't. A jolt from the past sometimes does the trick.'

'Shouldn't think he'd want to remember *his* past,' the corporal grinned, 'though I guess it can't be pleasant, gettin' the rope and not recallin' what you did wrong.'

At that moment the wagon stopped and from the sounds Otis heard it seemed the entire column was calling a halt. 'Stopping for the noon rest,' Fitzroy explained; then to the corporal he said, 'Go to the adjutant. Tell him the patient has recovered consciousness, and that the general can see him when it's convenient.'

'Yessir. Can't see why the general's so dawgone interested in him. Still, it ain't for the likes o' me to ask him.'

* * *

Lieutenant-Colonel George Armstrong Custer of the ripe-corn curls and sweeping dragoon's moustache, known as 'General' because of the rank he'd held during the Civil War, had left his command earlier that morning to go hunting, a sport he loved. He was very satisfied with the achievements of his expedition, and with the morning's hunt. He'd bagged a young roe-buck and a brace of fine quail. When he returned, he was irked by the sight of lawmen lingering impatiently about his wagons, but his mood lifted with the news that Fitzroy's patient had recovered consciousness. Custer smiled. The case intrigued him — and it seemed matters were falling most encouragingly into his lap.

For a moment, his mind dwelt on what had happened prior to embarking on this expedition. He had been on a visit to Chicago and had called into the offices of his old friend Alan Pinkerton, a dour Scot. The latter's detective agency was proving highly successful. As they smoked cigars, he told Custer a strange story, how one of his operatives, a man called Willis Grant, had been sent on a highly dangerous mission, the nature of which he was to reveal to no one, not even his wife Josephine, not even any other law authorities.

Grant was to pose as a convict, sentenced for an evil crime. While imprisoned he was to make the acquaintance of the two men, Will Selby and Grinner Willoughby who had been convicted for relieving the government coffers of a huge pay-roll and had hidden the cash before being caught. Government officials were desperate to discover the location of the money.

Grant's task was to gain the confidence of these two men and subsequently engineer an escape, after which they would undoubtedly return to the loot. The escape was to be 'arranged' during the transfer of the prisoners to the newly built prison in Canby City.

All had gone well until a considerable delay in the construction of the new prison had occurred due to a dispute over workers' wages. The expected completion of the building had been put back some six months. Meanwhile, Grant had remained in prison until the escape was eventually contrived.

Custer had wondered why he was being told this strange story and queried this very point.

'Because,' Pinkerton explained, 'it's highly likely that Grant will be in the Black Hills. I'd like you to keep your eyes open for him during your expedition and bring him out if you can.'

The general smiled. The intrigue of the case appealed to him, although he realized that the chances of locating the operative in such a vast region were somewhat unlikely — but he was always willing to undertake any task that might enhance his reputation.

'How can I identify this man?' he asked.

Pinkerton reached into his drawer. 'I knew you'd ask that. His wife has gone nearly crazy, questioning me about her husband's fate. She was expecting him to be away for just a few weeks, but things have dragged on and I couldn't tell her what he was up to. She gave me this.' He passed to Custer a heart-shaped locket, the sort a lady would normally wear about her neck.

The general pressed the catch and viewed the two small portraits inside, his eye lingering on that of the woman.

'Quite a fine looking lass, isn't she?' Pinkerton commented. 'She's certainly got a will of her own.'

Custer smiled approvingly. 'I wonder how she came to marry such a kink-nosed character?'

Now the general hurried through the camp, waving a casual acknowledgement to the men he passed as they straightened up and saluted him. Woe betide them if they failed to pay their respects!

Soon he was climbing into the ambulance, gesturing the corporal to leave himself and the doctor alone with the patient.

'Claims he's lost his memory,' Fitzroy explained. 'From the wound he took on his head, I can quite believe it.'

Custer nodded.

Otis, still cuffed to his bed, was sitting up, wondering why such interest blazed from the blue eyes of his high-ranking visitor. Custer rummaged in his satchel, took out some papers. He turned to Otis. 'Does the name Willis Grant, Pinkerton detective, mean anything to you?'

Otis shook his head, puzzled. 'Never heard of him.'

Custer cleared his throat. 'Well, in view of your amnesia, I guess that's not surprising. I'll explain things to you.' And he related the story Pinkerton had told to him.

Otis opened his mouth but said nothing.

The general was nodding as if to give credibility to his story. 'And this,' he went on, raising the open locket for Otis to see, 'is Willis Otis Grant.' He revealed only the right-sided portrait, keeping his thumb over the other picture.

Otis gazed in astonishment. 'That's me,' he gasped.

'Precisely,' Custer said.

Otis was dazed. He wondered if he was dreaming. Was the whole affair some nightmare . . . and would Rachel suddenly wake him up demanding to be kissed?

Custer's voice was prodding at him. 'You, my friend, are Willis Grant, Pinkerton detective and former medical student.'

'Can't be,' Otis murmured.

'It's in your interest to believe me,' Custer said. 'Otherwise I'll have to hand you over to the sheriff. No doubt he'd arrange you a fair trial and hanging.'

Otis's hard-pressed brain was racing. 'So there's no such real person as Otis Lockhart, no such woman-killer? And the escape was a put-up job?'

'Correct. But I have to congratulate you on the way you played the part. You convinced a lot of people.'

Otis could do no more than shake his head in bewilderment, but the warmth of relief was flooding through him. 'I even convinced myself,' he at last commented.

'Alan Pinkerton's an old friend of mine,' the general continued. 'He figured if you were still alive, you'd be in the Black Hills. So I promised to keep an eye open for you during this expedition. Good job I did, eh? And tell me: did you discover where the cash was hidden?'

Otis was so distracted by what had been revealed, that Custer had to repeat the question to reclaim his attention.

Otis remembered Rachel's map, given her by Charlie Casement, and the way it was buried with her. One day, it seemed, her body would have to be disturbed. One day, he promised himself, he would have it buried in a proper place, with a proper reverend speaking words. 'I have information about location of the cash,' he said. 'Under the circumstances, I'll pass it over personally to Alan Pinkerton.'

Custer looked faintly disappointed but he said, 'That's your prerogative, I guess. There's something else you'd better know. The fact that Alan Pinkerton has moved heaven and earth to find you, is due to a certain woman. She drove him near crazy, there in Chicago, visiting his office every day. Do you know who she is?' He passed Otis the locket, enjoying the game he was playing.

Otis gazed at the woman in the picture. She was holding her head slightly to one side, her fair hair curling to frame a face of calm symmetry, her full lips faintly pursed in readiness to smile. He touched her face with his finger.

Recollection was flowing into his mind like sand through a reluctant egg-timer. He felt breathless. When at last he spoke, his voice had a heedfulness about it as though dealing with something immensely precious. 'It's Josephine . . . my wife.'

Custer allowed himself a smile. 'Some women can be outstandingly loyal. I guess us men don't deserve such loyalty.' He raised a conspiratorial eyebrow. 'Anyway, I think it's high time I got my farrier to cut those handcuffs off you. Sheriff Rainbird and his bloodhounds are surely going to be disappointed when I give them the news. You're looking pretty rough after that surgery. Get some rest. You've got plenty of recovering to do, Willis Otis Grant.'

★ ★ ★

By the time Otis was brought into Fort Abraham Lincoln, he had suffered a setback. The bullet hole in his chest had got infected and, as fever burned in him, his life had hung in the balance. What pulled him through, in addition to Fitzroy's skills, was his determination to live. Having survived all that fate could throw at him in the Black Hills, he balked at the prospect of meeting up with Holy Jack amid the fires of Hades.

Josephine hastened from Chicago as soon as Alan Pinkerton informed her that her husband had been traced and was recovering from his wounds in the fort's hospital. She travelled by rail and stage coach, making her first excursion into the West.

On the day she was due to arrive, Otis was sufficiently recovered to have a hair-cut and beard-trim. He felt like a beau going on his first date, instead of a married man being reunited with his wife. There were still gaps in his memory, particularly those relating to his personal life, although he spent much time staring at the picture of Josephine, trying to build on the vague, comforting feeling it gave him. He also pondered a great deal on the Pinkerton Detective Agency, his employers. Alan Pinkerton had telegraphed him with congratulations on the outcome of his mission, saying that he could take all the time he needed to recuperate.

For some strange reason, his most vivid recollections revolved around his childhood on the family ranch, his days at medical college, his qualification as a doctor and his final quitting of the profession because he had failed to save the life of his ailing father. All that had been before he joined Alan Pinkerton.

Now, he sat at the hospital window, sunlight streaming in as he watched for the coach to arrive. In his lap was a copy of the *Bismark Gazette*, the print so large it filled the whole of the front page:

CUSTER LOCATES GOLD
IN THE BLACK HILLS

243

★

Nuggets pulled up with GRASS ROOTS
Wild Excitement
Among The Troops!

★

THE NEW LANDS OF PROMISE!

★

Prepare for Exciting Times!

He wondered if the Indians had read the news.

The trumpeter at the guard gate sounded the noon mess call, and presently he heard the clatter of dishes. Heat hazed the windless air. The coach was already a half-hour late. He wondered if Josephine was making out all right and if he'd be capable of picking up the threads of their marriage. Would he be able to put behind him all the trauma he'd suffered — and the memory of his love for Rachel? No, he corrected himself, it hadn't been *his* love. It had been Johnny No Name's. And Johnny No Name was gone now. It was as if he was dead, riding in the sky with Rachel, maybe at last showing her about all those sins of the flesh she had craved for.

The only identity he now possessed was that of Willis Otis Grant, but he was a shadow of that once stocky man, his face moon-pale with sombre lines carved into it like scars. Yet at least he was alive and he had been granted the time to regain his health, physically and mentally.

He pushed himself up from his chair, excitement stirring him. The coach had pulled in on the far side of the parade square, the four horses raising a cloud of dust as the driver hauled back on his reins and applied the brake. Otis watched two men dismount. One of them turned to help a lady step down, her dress a radiant blue, and seeing her was like a great weight being lifted from his shoulders . . . Josephine. Suddenly memories, sweet memories, were filling the gaps in his mind. Soon she was ushered in, her face filled with compassion. As they embraced, he knew that her presence would be like a beacon, burning brightly and illuminating the future with healing, understanding and renewed hope.

THE END

THE CROOKED SHERIFF
John Dyson

Black Pete Bowen quit Texas with a burning hatred of men who try to take the law into their own hands. But he discovers that things aren't much different in the silver mountains of Arizona.

THEY'LL HANG BILLY FOR SURE: LARRY & STRETCH
Marshall Grover

Billy Reese, the West's most notorious desperado, was to stand trial. From all compass points came the curious and the greedy, the riff-raff of the frontier. Suddenly, a crazed killer was on the loose — but the Texas Trouble-Shooters were there, girding their loins for action.

RIDERS OF RIFLE RANGE
Wade Hamilton

Veterinarian Jeff Jones did not like open warfare — but it was there on Scrub Pine grass. When he diagnosed a sick bull on the Endicott ranch as having the contagious blackleg disease, he got involved in the warfare — whether he liked it or not!

THE WEST WITCH
Lance Howard

Detective Quinton Hilcrest journeys west, seeking the Black Hood Bandits' lost fortune. Within hours of arriving in Hags Bend, he is fighting for his life, ensnared with a beautiful outcast the town claims is a witch! Can he save the young woman from the angry mob?